RED VI
AND THE
SPELLBOUND STABLES

Also by Mo Kerr:

The Ice Cave Monster (illustrations by Nora Haikala)
The Giant Sunflower (illustrations by Nora Haikala)
Until Amy is Found

OSTRICH BOOKS

..Bury your head in a book.

www.ostrichbooks.co.uk

First published in Great Britain 2022
Copyright © Maureen Hanrahan 2022

ISBN 978-1-8382586-5-8

Printed by IngramSpark
Typeset and Designed by Kerrypress, St Albans, Markyate
Cover illustration by Nora Haikala

To my family

RED VIPEREEN
AND THE
SPELLBOUND STABLES

MO KERR

Ostrich Books

The Curse of Red Vipereen

After a good night's sleep, Madame Fosse was ravenous. Licking her lips at the thought of breakfast, she leapt out of bed. But, oh dear, her legs went from under her and, try as she might, she couldn't get to her feet.

'Help... Help!' she yelled at the top of her voice.

Palace residents running to the rescue, found their beloved psychic in a heap on the floor. With her black hair and black nightgown, she lay huffing and puffing like a beached whale. In the end, it took four stalwart guards to hoist her back onto the four-poster bed.

'What's wrong with me?' she wailed.

By the time Prince Rupert arrived in his flowing purple gown, Madame Fosse had worked herself up into a frenzy.

'I know who's behind this,' she screamed. 'RED VIPEREEN, that's who. And I bet you anything you like, he's the reason I haven't been able to get my Diviner working.'

At the mention of Red Vipereen, everyone fell silent and one by one they slunk out of the room leaving Prince

Rupert alone with Madame Fosse. The prince, his dark face tense with concern, paced up and down. 'I don't understand it. I really don't. The Permanent Seal Spell should have prevented that evil wizard getting anywhere near us.'

'Well, it hasn't, has it? Helmets and Damson Nation,' Madame Fosse exploded. 'Somehow that jiggery wizard's put a spell on me. My legs might never work again. I may be crippled for life. I might have to spend the rest of my days in a wheelchair.'

Prince Rupert passed a hand over his cropped, raven hair and surveyed Madame Fosse with sorrowful eyes. 'Oh dear, oh dear, this is all too much. Vipereen must be stopped in his tracks. The quicker we launch The Mission to find the Blessed Crystal, the better. The palace is doomed otherwise.'

'And how exactly are we supposed to find the Blessed Crystal when I can't get a lead from my Diviner? Vipereen's mucked it up good and proper.'

For three whole days Madame Fosse was unable to leave her bed but, on the fourth day, when Prince Rupert looked in to see how she was, she made another attempt to get out of bed and this time, miraculously, her legs did what they were supposed to do.

'I CAN STAND,' she cried, tottering across the room. 'I CAN WALK. THE CURSE IS BROKEN.' And, still in her nightgown, she raced out of the room and along the corridor to her Psychitoreum.

By the time Prince Rupert caught up with her, Madame Fosse was rubbing away at the gigantic screen of her

Diviner with the sleeve of her nightie. She winked at the prince. 'Let's see if it's back in action and what it's got to say for itself.' But although the palace psychic rubbed and rubbed, trying to clear a dense murk, nothing appeared. For half an hour she kept at it and was about to give up when the fog lifted, and a figure appeared.

'It's Wizard Grindsniff!'

Prince Rupert gasped. 'No...surely... It can't be... Are you sure?'

'It's really dim, but it's Grindsniff all right. There's no mistaking his wizardy image.'

'Well, bless me. Who would have thought?' The prince peered over the psychic's shoulder but couldn't see a thing. 'Are you sure?'

'Of course I'm sure. You don't possess the gift, that's why you can't see anything.'

'Our old friend's still alive, then? That's wonderful.'

'I'm not so sure he's alive, but he's definitely trying to send a message. Only the image keeps breaking up. He's trying so hard, so hard to get through. But wait... No, surely not...?' Madame Fosse looked as if she'd been whacked by a gorilla. 'I can't believe it. I can't believe it,' she murmured.

'What is it? What is he saying?'

'Sshh... He's talking about a boy. Some boy. Eleven years old. Grindsniff is saying he's the one who can help us.'

'Well, bless me.' Prince Rupert scratched his princely head. 'Are you sure? Are you sure this isn't another of Red Vipereen's dastardly tricks?'

'Oh no.' Madame Fosse whispered. 'This is no trick. But that's not all. The boy is in mortal danger because Vipereen already has him in his sights.'

'So, where is this boy?' Prince Rupert demanded. 'We must save him. Find him at once.'

'Grindsniff's trying to say something, but, oh no, it's misting up again. There, it's gone. Vipereen's curse must still be lingering.' Madame Fosse got to her feet to make sure her legs were still working, then sat down again. 'We have a real problem on our hands, Prince Rupert. This boy can help us in some way, but we haven't a clue as to who or where he is. She rubbed frantically at the screen. 'Come on, come on, Grindsniff. Try and get through.' But the screen remained a blank.

Caws Calling

Jack Goodchild stared out of the window at a sky filled with stars. 'Tonight's story is about Grumblestump, Heard of Grumblestump, either of you?'

'No, 'cos you just made it up,' Holly said.

'You think so? Well, let me tell you, Grumblestump was real enough. He was a giant with a rumbly, thundery voice, and legs so long he could cross the world in a couple of strides, and he was so big that when he lifted his arms, he could touch the stars. Monsters and dragons didn't stand a chance when Grumblestump went after them. But the strangest thing of all...' Jack Goodchild had to raise his voice because of a great roaring noise coming from outside.

'What's going on?' Holly sat bolt upright as a flash of red light hurtled past the window.

Jack Goodchild was too carried away with his story '...the strangest thing of all about Grumblestump was his eyes. Big as cauldrons they were and that's not all. He had this knack, you see, of making one eye go deep inside his head so that even a heron couldn't reach it and sticking the other one out and swivelling it round and round.'

Edwin dived under the bedclothes with a strangled 'aargh...!'

'You've done it again, Dad,' Holly sighed. 'He's never going to get to sleep now. You know he hates all that scary stuff.'

Coming back down to earth, Jack Goodchild smiled. 'Good job you don't frighten easily, Tinker Bell.'

Why Dad always called her Tinker Bell, Holly had no idea. Built like a tank, flaming red candyfloss hair and a face full of freckles, wasn't exactly fairy-like. And it was all Dad's fault because everyone said she looked like him. How she wished she looked more like Edwin with his pixie face, pale skin and silver-blond hair, just like Mum. It was all the wrong way round.

'So, there's another good story ruined.' Jack Goodchild said. 'And I can't think of anything else off the top of my head, Tink, but not to worry, I'll come up with something for tomorrow. Now, off to sleep the pair of you.'

After Jack Goodchild lumbered off downstairs, whistling tunelessly, the room fell quiet, so quiet that voices floated up from the street below. Holly clambered over her bed to the window and peered out. As she did so, another flash of red lit up the whole room, so powerful this time, that for a second Holly was blinded. (Edwin was still deep under the bedcovers.) Holly watched as a glowing red speck receded and was swallowed up by the night. But down in the street, there was another strange sight. A black Rolls Royce was parked under a streetlamp; beside it, two men in long black coats and black top hats. But it was the two women they were talking to that riveted Holly's attention. Both were thin as rakes with noses like daggers, black straggly hair and skimpy black skirts, black leather jackets and boots. *They look like twins.* Holly thought. *Twin witches!*

The idea had no sooner popped into Holly's head than the two women swung round and stared straight up at her. Holly threw herself back on the bed.

But curiosity getting the better of her, she went to take another look and was in time to see the women leap onto motorbikes and roar off. At the end of the road, the bikes lifted off the ground and soared into the air.

Holly rubbed her eyes. *Was she dreaming?*

'What're you looking at, sis?' Edwin said, finally emerging.

'Nothing.' Holly pulled the curtains to and scrambled back into bed. 'Just go to sleep.'

'Could Grumblestump really do that?' Edwin asked in a trembly voice.

'What, that thing with his eyes? Don't be daft' Holly retorted. 'As if anyone could ever do that. It's just one of Dad's stories. Nothing like that happens in real life.'

'Even millions and trillions of years ago?'

Holly yawned.

I bet there are monsters and dragons. Even giants,' Edwin persisted.

'Oh, for goodness sake, Ed, shut up. I'm going to sleep so you might as well do the same.'

Holly didn't go to sleep. She forced herself to stay awake, at least until she was certain Edwin wasn't lying shaking with fear. That didn't mean he wouldn't wake up in the middle of the night screaming his head off about 'eyes'.

Holly was sick of always looking out for her brother. But what choice did she have when Mum kept going on about how delicate he was with his asthma. Except it was no joke because there was that one time she'd seen him having an attack in the playground. As he struggled to breathe, she thought he wouldn't make it. Ever since, she always checked he had his inhaler with him.

She tried wrapping the thin duvet tight around her body to keep out the draughts. When it rained and the wind was blowing in a certain direction, water dripped steadily from a corner of the ceiling. Mum was forever getting onto the landlord, but nothing got fixed. It wasn't fair, Holly thought. Mum worked so hard as a waitress in a local café. How many times had she said, 'Oh, if only your father could get a job, but he's so unlucky. Or if only I could get a better job. We'd be able to patch things up ourselves.'

Holly couldn't understand why her father couldn't get a job. Once, on a visit to see Uncle Tom and Aunt Bridget, she'd overheard her aunt say, "If you want my opinion, Jack lives in a world of his own. He belongs in Disney Land. He doesn't understand people. No wonder he can't hold a job down.'

The next day on their way home from Barford Comprehensive school, Holly saw the black Rolls again. This time, parked at the end of their street.

'Wow, look at that,' Edwin said. 'That must belong to someone rich.'

'No one round here then,' Holly said.

When Edwin tried to peer inside the tinted windows, Holly yanked him away.

'D'you think we'll ever get to have a ride in a car like that?' Edwin asked.

'Don't be daft.'

'But Dad said he was going to buy a Rolls one day and treat us to high tea at The Swan.' The Swan was the poshest hotel in Barford.

'That's just dad making stuff up again.'

'Well, one day I'm going to treat us all to tea at The Swan.' Edwin said. 'You'll see.'

Holly giggled. 'You're as bad as Dad, you are.'

The following day, they walked past the black Rolls again, this time parked nearer to their house.

On Friday afternoon it was there again and once more Holly had to stop Edwin from peering inside. 'I wish we were rich,' he snapped. 'I'd be able to have a horse if we were rich.'

'A horse? Where'd you get that crazy idea? Holly said. 'What would you do with a horse?'

Edwin scowled at her.

No sooner were they through the front door than Holly knew something was wrong. It was the way Mum looked at them or didn't look at them. The way she was all unsmiling and droopy. And there was the mail still strewn across the hall floor. Holly gathered everything up – bills by the looks – and set them on the rickety hall table. Edward was always saying he wanted a horse, but Holly had her heart set on a dog: a big friendly, sloppy dog, like some of her friends had; a dog that would come bounding up to meet her.

Edwin shrugged off his jacket and schoolbag and plonked them on the floor; still in a huff over the car business, Holly decided. She picked up the jacket and hung it beside her own on a coat hook and placed his bag beside her own in the corner.

In the kitchen, she watched as her mother set about making their tea. Normally, Alice Goodchild did everything in a rush, as if there wasn't a second to lose. Things were never ever tidied away: drawers weren't closed properly, things left poking out and stuff tumbled out of cupboards when you opened them. There was never even enough time to get all the tangles out of Holly's frizzy hair. But today was very different. Alice Goodchild was moving as if in a trance. Usually, toast was in and out of the toaster before developing a tan. Not today. Holly watched as her mother scraped black bits off the burned toast and slowly spread marmite over the scaly surface. Luckily the marmite helped disguise the burnt taste. And where was Dad? He was usually always there at teatime, asking how school had gone.

After tea, Edwin said he had some spellings to learn and dragged himself upstairs. Holly was so worried about her mother she decided to help with the washing-up and do her maths homework later. It was while they were stood side by side at the kitchen sink that Alice Goodchild suddenly burst into tears. 'It's your dad,' she said. 'He's gone and left us.'

'What d'you mean, gone?' Holly said, trying to keep her voice steady. 'He wouldn't just go off without seeing us.'

Mrs Goodchild cried even harder. 'He's gone and got himself a job abroad. Someone phoned after you'd gone to school wanting him to start straight away. Some kind of decorating job. I'm not sure what. I don't know that he knew himself. He didn't want to leave us, but what choice did he have? He's tried and tried to get a job round here, but it's hopeless.' She wiped her eyes on a tea towel. 'He's off to some isolated part of Iceland, where it's so cold he might freeze to death. He said the money was good, but what's the use of that if he ends up with frostbite.'

'Oh, he'll be fine, you'll see, Holly said matter-of-factly but, inside, she wasn't feeling at all matter-of-fact. What was everyone at school going to say? They'd probably think Dad had just got fed up and dumped them. They wouldn't know Dad would never do a thing like that.'

Over the next few weeks, Holly had her work cut out going around holding her head high, as if she were descended from royalty. Whenever anyone at school said anything about her dad having run off, she gave them a dirty look and a flash of her emerald eyes that Mum said could kill a person stone dead a mile away. It would have helped if they'd had a letter or even a postcard from Dad, but there'd been nothing. Things were so bad Mum had

had to take on cleaning jobs on top of her waitressing to make ends meet. She kept saying she was tired, and she looked it.

One Sunday, Holly helped make the dinner. Mum was nearly back to normal, doing everything at double speed. The sausages looked a bit anaemic, and the mashed potatoes still had lumps in. It was as she was thrashing the spinach, green bits flying up and sticking to her face, that she said: 'If ever things get too bad for us, Holly, at least we'll always have a roof over our heads with your Uncle Tom and Bridget in Strawbridge.'

Holly had just decided things couldn't get any worse when they did. One afternoon, during playtime, she rescued Edwin from a couple of bullies who were punching and kicking him. His knee sprouting red bobbles, Holly was leading him towards the first-aid room when she spotted the black Rolls gliding past the school gates and, when they arrived home, there it was again, parked right outside their house. Holly had a real sense of dread.

She rang the doorbell. She rang again and again, banged on the door, but it remained shut. It was then she heard the footsteps. Swinging round, she saw two black-coated men, one tall, one short, walking towards them. The tall man doffed his top hat and said they were from the Ministry of CAWS.

'Afraid I've got some bad news,' he said. 'Something came up. Your mother's had to leave town.'

When Edwin started bawling, Holly had to choke back tears so as not to make things worse. But her head was spinning. Where could Mum have possibly gone? Only that morning she'd waved them goodbye. Why hadn't she come by the school to let them know she was going away? It wasn't like Mum to just go off without saying a word. Supposing these horrid men were lying?

'Where's she gone?' Holly asked.

The men shook their heads. 'We don't know.'

'But she'd never just go off. Has something happened to Dad?'

No reply.

'So, what do you want with us?' Holly demanded.

'We've come to take you into custody,' the tall man said.

Holly didn't like the sound of that. 'What Ministry did you say you were from?'

'The Ministry of CAWS.' The short man said, and he spelt it out. 'C..A..W..S.'

'Like crows do, you mean?' The men did look like crows. 'What does CAWS mean?'

'Children Alone Without Support'

'Well, that doesn't apply to us, then,' Holly flung back. 'Cos we're not alone. Our Dad'll be back any minute. And Mum as well.'

The tall crow bent towards her, poking his beaky nose into her face. 'Where is your father?'

'He's got a job in Iceland,' Edwin blurted out before Holly could stop him. 'I bet you anything that's where Mum's gone.'

The two crows exchanged knowing glances. One of them tried a smile that nearly cracked his face.

'Then you'll have to come with us till your mother or father gets back.'

This set Edwin off again. Holly threw the crows a stony look. 'Mum said we were never to go with strangers, so if you don't mind, Edwin and I will be quite all right, thank you.'

'What's your dad's address?'

'That's none of your business,' Holly said.

'And you'd better be careful.' Edwin said in a trembly voice. 'Our dad's a big man. A sort of giant.'

'That's right. So, if anything happens to us, he'll kill you. So don't say we didn't warn you.'

The short crow peered at Holly. 'That's enough of this nonsense, little miss. You're to come with us to the Holding Bay. Your Mum or Dad can collect you there. That's if they ever do come back.'

Holly wasn't used to being pushed around. 'How do we know you're from the Ministry of Caws? I've never heard of it. You could be kidnappers in disguise.'

The tall crow held out an identity card. Holly stared at it hard. She turned it over to look at the back. It looked like the real thing. A long face and squinty eyes just like the tall crow stared up at her and stamped right across the card was a blurry, purplish word: **OFFICIAL**

Holly was still studying the card when the short crow made a grab for Edwin with hands the size of shovels. The tall one then lunged towards Holly.

'Oh no you don't,' Holly ducked out of reach, spun round and landed a kick on the crow's shin. She was all set to race off down the road, when she saw Edwin being bundled into the Rolls. Now what was she supposed to do? Run and get help? Leave Edwin at the mercy of these crows? Mum would never forgive her... Holly barrelled into one of the crows, arms and legs flailing. 'Let him go. D'you hear? Let him go,' she screamed.

One of the crows grabbed her and, before she knew it, she was shoved into the car alongside her brother who was huddled in a heap, sobbing.

Holly shouted and banged on the window. 'Let us out of here. Let us out. Where are you taking us?'

There was no reply as the black Rolls Royce silently sped away.

Hell at Holding Bay

The car pulled up outside a large, redbrick house. Set apart from the other houses in the road, it was the horridest, ugliest building Holly had ever seen. With black brickwork and barred windows, it resembled a prison.

'Here we are,' the tall crow said. 'Out you get. This is the Holding Bay. Here's where you'll stay till things get sorted.'

'We're only carrying out orders,' the short crow said as if feeling a bit sorry for them.

An old woman, dressed all in white, opened the door. A white porridge face was all smiles and tiny blue eyes twinkled like fairy lights.

Large baguette arms reached out to hug them. 'Welcome, my dears. I am so sorry to hear about your mother going off and leaving you, but don't worry, we'll look after you until she comes back. You must call me Aunt Winifred.'

Holly had to bite her lip to stop herself crying. Edwin, she could tell, was too frightened to even cry because, although Aunt Winifred seemed all right, the inside of the house was dark and gloomy. Holly swung round to tell the crows to take them back home, but the men and the Rolls had disappeared.

'I expect you're hungry.' Aunt Winifred led them into a vast, high-ceilinged kitchen full of women wearing black mini-skirts, fish-net tights and shocking-pink tank tops. They looked exactly like the two women Holly had seen outside her house. There were loads of them, all with dark eyes, pointed noses, black hair and arms tattooed with red snakes.

Black cauldrons, like giant cockroaches, hung down from the ceiling and a whole wall was covered in broomsticks thick with cobwebs. Globules of grease crawled down the walls like fat caterpillars and all the worktops were piled high were dirty dishes. There were so many people crowded into the kitchen that everyone had to shuffle this way just to move a few inches. Holly and Edwin were made to shuffle along to a table to sit alongside some other children. No sooner had they sat down than bowls of soup and glasses of orange juice were plonked in front of them.

'Yuk, it's horrid.' Edwin spat out his first mouthful of soup.

'Ssshh,' Holly whispered. 'Try and get some of it down.'

The other children were pulling faces. The soup was bright green with bits of cabbage floating on top and it smelled of rotten onions. But with sharp noses pointed in their direction, all the children squeezed a few more drops down their throats and washed the taste away with water.

Holly and Edwin had to wait behind when the other children left the kitchen.

'I'm starving,' Edwin said.

'Just be quiet, or you'll be for it,' Holly whispered fiercely.

One of the women led them up two flights of stairs and into a bathroom. They were handed pyjamas and told to wash, after which they were shown into a large room with a long row of narrow beds.

The woman pointed to two empty beds. 'Into bed, and not a peep out of you till morning,' she warned, in a voice as cracked and dry as a desert.

As soon as the two women had left, Edwin started whimpering about wanting to go home.

'Sshh,' Holly whispered. 'They said not to make a noise. Don't make things worse.'

'They're witches,' came a clear voice. Holly made out a small, curly-haired girl sitting up in bed.

Holly nodded. 'I guessed as much. I saw two of them outside our house a few nights ago. But I thought witches had long black skirts, pointed hats. And black cats.'

'They changed their style years ago,' the girl said. 'There are definitely no cats. But they *are* witches. Did you see all the broomsticks in the kitchen?'

'Looked like they hadn't been used for years...'

'They haven't. They're old-fashioned. Now they have motorbikes. Harley Davidsons. They say they're a lot better for getting around in the sky and on the ground.'

Holly recalled the motorbikes she'd seen outside her house. So maybe she hadn't imagined them taking to the sky, after all.

'Did you say the sky?' Edwin chimed in.

'Keep your voice down, Ed,' Holly warned.

'Yes, but motorbikes can't fly.'

'The ones they have can,' the girl said.

'Does Aunt Winifred have one?' Holly couldn't picture the sweet, old lady on a motorbike. 'Is she a witch as well?'

'No, I don't think she's one of them,' the girl said. 'She's just bonkers or else they've put a spell on her.'

'What's your name?' Holly asked. 'And how long have you been here?'

'Emily. But we should stop talking 'cos they'll be back any minute.'

When Edwin started snuffling, Holly told him to shut up. She lay quite still, unable to sleep. Five minutes later she heard the bedroom door open and made out two dark shapes. She closed her eyes and held her breath sensing the witches going from one bed to the other. When footsteps stopped by her bed, Holly felt stinking, cold breath on her face. She prayed Edwin wouldn't wake up.

The next day and the day after that, Holly and Edwin were made to work non-stop dusting and polishing non-stop.

'If only we could be back home,' Edwin said.

One day they were given the job of scrubbing all the floors with buckets of icy water. In no time, Edwin was out of breath and feeling faint. When a witch pushed by them, Holly decided she'd had enough. 'It's not fair,' she protested. 'My brother has asthma.'

And we're having to work much harder than the others,' Edwin complained. 'We shouldn't even be here.'

'You're here because Red Vipereen wants you here,' the witch barked. 'So do as you're told and keep out of mischief. See.' She prodded Holly in the chest. 'See...' Another prod.

Holly stood her ground. 'Who is this Red Vipereen? And why does he want us here?'

'You'll find out soon enough. Now, get on with it and don't try any funny business.' The witch kicked out, sending Holly's bucket of water sploshing everywhere.'

'Now look what you've made me do?' the witch screamed. 'Get this mess cleaned up. RIGHT AWAY.'

After scrubbing every floor in the house, except the kitchen, Holly and Edwin were given a mountain of washing and ironing to do. Holly did most of it because Edwin was exhausted. It wasn't fair, she kept telling herself. Why had the witches got it in for the two of them?

Over the days ahead, Edwin went around with a dopey look in his eyes, as if he didn't know what day it was. Most of the children were like zombies as well, even if they didn't work half as hard. At least Emily and her friend Michael, a podgy boy with wire-framed glasses, had a bit more spark.

'Do you know who Red Vipereen is?' Holly asked Emily.

Emily nodded. 'He's a weirdo wizard.'

'A wizard!' Holly exclaimed. 'But...'

'Yes, he really is a wizard,' Emily said.

'The creepiest one there is,' Michael added. 'He dresses in this tight red suit and has this red beard down to his feet and he's got snake's eyes. I reckon he *is* a snake, in disguise.'

'And every time he arrives, someone disappears,' Emily said.

'They end up in a dungeon,' Michael said, his eyes on Edwin who was whimpering with fear. 'And get tortured to death.'

Edwin started crying.

'That's not what happens at all,' Emily said. 'You shouldn't keep upsetting Edwin.'

'So, what does happen?' Holly said.

'They end up as servants for retired witches,' Emily said. 'I know because a girl called Joanne disappeared and then came back. She said the witch she worked for died, so Vipereen brought her back, till another vacancy came up.'

'Yes, but what about the prisoners locked in the cellar,' Michael said, eyes still fixed on Edwin. 'We've seen the witches taking food down.'

I did hear them talking about an escaped prisoner, once,' Emily said. 'But I've never actually seen them taking anyone down there.'

The next time Holly saw Aunt Winifred she demanded to know where the children went after leaving the Holding Bay. Aunt Winifred beamed and told her they went to foster homes and that Holly and her brother would soon be found a new home as well.

'What are they like, these foster homes?' Holly asked.

'Oh, I'm sure they're very nice,' Aunt Winifred assured her. 'Every bit as nice and cosy as here.'

Holly groaned. 'And what about the people they go to? I suppose they're as nice as everyone here?'

Aunt Winifred smiled. 'Oh, every bit as nice. Every bit, my dear.'

It was all too much for Holly. 'Well, Edwin and I won't be going anywhere, thank you very much,' she snapped. ''Cos this place is horrid and the witches stink.'

'Oh my, oh my. I'm sure you don't really mean that,' Aunt Winfred looked about to faint.

A few days later as Holly was washing a stack of smelly fishnet tights in the laundry room, she heard voices in the corridor. She tiptoed to the door and peeked out. A witch was talking to a funny looking man dressed all in red, with a red beard down to his toes and eyes like a snake. Not only that, but words came hissing out of his mouth, just like a snake. Red Vipereen. No doubt about it.

'Goodchilds giving any trouble?' Vipereen hissed.

Holly stifled a gasp.

'The girl's a handful.' the witch replied, 'but the boy's as meek as a lamb.'

'Ready for slaughter, then?' Vipereen's hissy laugh sent a shiver down Holly's spine. 'Still, watch your step with him. He's the one with special powers.' Red Vipereen's thin body shimmered with laughter.

Holly wondered if she was hearing right. Special powers? Edwin?

'Hard to believe there's anything special about that little weed,' the witch cackled. 'Least bit of work knocks him out. His sister says he has asthma. Still, bet you were pleased to get your hands on the pair?'

Vipereen let out a great hiss of steam. 'Light years ahead of the other party, that's why. They haven't got Wizard Grindsniff to help them anymore.' Another hiss. 'Fool. Thinking he could take on the Wastelands. And now we have the boy, and my plans are almost ready. Watch them day and night, d'you hear? Because if anything goes wrong...' The words petered out with a menacing hiss.

'What'll happen to the two of them eventually?' the witch asked.

This time the hiss was bloodcurdling. 'I have plans for them. Experiments in mind. Ha, ha, ha...'

Holly shrank back into the furthest corner of the room, trying to make herself invisible.

For the rest of the day, she kept going over and over what she'd heard. Red Vipereen's voice hammered in her brain. *I have plans for them. Experiments in mind.*

Terrified though she was, Holly didn't say anything to Edwin. Instead, she kept trying to come up with an escape plan. That night, Holly lay in bed listening to Edwin sobbing his heart out. When she told him to stop crying, his sobs got even louder. Two witches came and carted him off in a sack.

Edwin was a quivering wreck the next morning.

'It was horrible. They locked me in this cupboard with all these cobwebs and there was this horrible smell. I had an asthma attack and I thought I was going to die.'

It was then that Holly remembered her mum's words. It was as if Mum was standing right next to her: *If ever things get too bad, Holly, at least we'll always have a roof over our heads with Tom and Bridget.*

'We're getting out of here, tonight, Ed,' she whispered, looking all around to make sure the coast was clear. 'And I know where we're going, as well.'

'Where?'

'To Strawbridge. We're going to Uncle Tom and Aunt Bridget's.'

Edwin still looked thoroughly miserable. 'But how are we going to get there? How are we going to get out of this place?'

'Just leave that to me,' Holly said.

Holly invited Emily and Michael to join in the escape, but they shook their heads. 'It's not a bit of use you even trying,' Emily said. 'The witches will only sniff you out and bring you back and punish you.'

Michael pushed his glasses up his nose. 'And you'll end up in a stew or something and we'll have to eat you.'

Edwin howled.

Look, take this,' Emily said and handed Holly a small bottle of perfume. 'It's called Cloud of Angels. My mum used to wear it, but you can have it. Dab a bit on and it might put the witches off your scent.

Holly waited until there had been the witch night inspection then climbed out of her bed and whispered to Edwin to get up and get dressed.

Before leaving the bedroom, Holly stuffed pillows under the sheets hoping it might fool the witches for a while. Tiptoeing over to the door, she looked out. The corridor was clear, and she beckoned to Edwin. Quickly they made their way to the bathroom at the end of the corridor. Holly locked the door and crossed to a high sash window, the only window in the whole house without bars. She pushed it open. Beneath the window was the flat roof of the kitchen and beneath that a backyard with moonlight glinting on dozens of Harley-Davidsons. It was a long drop to the kitchen roof, but Holly reckoned that by lowering yourself over the edge and hanging by your hands from the window ledge, it wouldn't be that big a drop. She knew she could manage it, but what about Edwin?

'Edwin,' she gave him a fierce look. 'Do you want to stay in this rotten dump for the rest of your life?'

Edwin shook his head.

'Then you've got to be brave. Okay. Watch what I do, then copy me.'

Knowing there was no time to lose Holly clambered up onto the window ledge and lowered herself over the edge. She looked up into Edwin's terrified eyes. 'See how easy it is?'

Holly dropped with a small thud onto the tarmac roof and signalled for Edwin to follow.

Edwin shook his head.

'Come on,' Holly ordered in a fierce whisper. 'It's easy peasy. If you don't do it, I'll murder you.'

One leg appeared over the windowsill before Edwin clambered back inside.

Holly was furious. Any minute now and a witch might catch them. 'Edwin Goodchild, if you don't get down here I...I...I'll...well I'll leave you here.' She marched to the edge of the flat roof as if intending to leave him behind.

'Don't go, sis.' Edwin begged.

'Keep your voice down. Well, are you coming or not? Just climb out and let yourself drop. I'll catch you.'

Once again, a leg appeared, but this time, Edwin's body followed. He was whimpering.

'Oh, come on, Ed. Be a hero. Jump! Jump! I'm standing right here waiting to catch you.'

He jumped, landed on his feet and gave a victory whoop. Holly clamped a hand over his mouth. 'Sshh. Didn't I say you could do it. Now come on. We're not out of the woods yet.'

From the flat roof to the ground was a long drop. Edwin pointed to a drainpipe running down the side. 'We could climb down that.'

'Okay, Spiderman, show me how it's done.'

And to Holly's amazement, he did, shinning down the pipe as nimble as a monkey. Fast as she could, Holly followed suit. There was not a minute to lose.

They ran swiftly across the backyard weaving in and out of the motorbikes until they reached the street, then ran as fast as they could past several blocks of houses, past shops, banks and tall office blocks, all barred and bolted for the night. Holly had no idea where they were going. Just so long as they could get as far away from the Holding Bay as possible. But Edwin was finding it hard to breathe.

'I can't run anymore,' he complained. 'I'm out of breath.'

'Take a few deep breaths.'

I can't help it, Holly. I'm going to have one of my attacks.'

'Just try to run a bit further. Come on.'

They had not run more than a few more yards when Edwin gave up. 'It's no good, Holly.' He pointed to his chest. 'I can hardly breathe.'

Edwin had turned white and was struggling to breathe. Holly pulled him into a shop doorway, and they huddled down at the far end for a rest.

'Take some more deep breaths,' she said. 'Try and relax.'

Edwin was just beginning to breathe normally when a huge clap of thunder broke out only the thunder didn't die away as it was supposed to. Instead, it got louder and louder. When it reached the front of the shop, Holly realised what it was.

'Motorbikes, Edwin,' she whispered. 'It's the witches and they might sniff us out.'

A Whiff of Things to Come

Remembering the perfume Emily had given her, Holly dug it out of her pocket.

'We'll have to give this a go,' she said, dabbing *Cloud of Angels* on her wrists and behind her ears, the way she'd seen it done in films. The scent of melon and roses hung in the air. When she tried to dab some on Edwin, he jerked away.

'I don't want any of that stuff on.'

'Oh, don't be stupid...'

As Holly began dabbing scent behind Edwin's ears, she sensed his thin body stiffen. Swinging round, she was in time to see two witches, pointed noses raised, sniffing the air inside the doorway.

The witches inched further and further inside, peering and sniffing. Smelling something, but what? If Edwin started yelling... So, once again, Holly clamped a hand over his mouth, just in case.

Now whether it was the perfume that put them off the scent, or whether the witches' eyesight wasn't up to much, Holly didn't know, but after sniff sniffing the doorway for several minutes, they turned and disappeared.

When they were quite sure the witches had gone, the pair ventured out. Dawn was breaking. Mail and newspapers were being delivered. It was a cold day, the wind sharp and penetrating. Holly wished they had their coats, but as soon as they'd arrived at the Holding Bay, their coats had been whisked away. At the end of a street there was a sign pointing to Barford railway station and Holly remembered the train rides they'd taken with their parents to Strawbridge.

By now there were lots of people around, people opening up shops or making their way to work, but although it made them feel safer, Holly still kept a sharp lookout for witches, or Harley Davidsons. It was only when they reached the station that Holly remembered she had no money to buy tickets.

'Now what do we do?' Holly muttered to herself.

'What did you say?'

'Nothing,' Holly said. 'Let's just sit down for a minute while I think.'

She led Edwin over to a bench inside the station.

'I'm hungry and cold. And I'm tired.'

'And I'm not, I suppose,' Holly snapped.

'I wish Mum was here to look after us.'

'Well, she's not,' Holly said. 'So, you'll just have to make do with me.'

People were going in and out of the station non-stop. Holly toyed with the idea of just marching up to someone and asking them to buy their tickets, but then very quickly dismissed the idea. Mum had always warned her about talking to strangers; also, people might wonder what two kids were doing asking for money. They'd be sure to contact CAWS and the crows would be sent to round them up. The witches would probably kill them for running away. Perhaps it would be best to forget about a train and try and walk instead. Holly turned to look at Edwin and found him slumped at her side, fast asleep. Strawbridge was a long way away. Holly had no idea of how far, but it had to be miles. No way would Edwin be able to make it.

Holly was very cross with herself because she wasn't usually stumped for ideas. Her mind a complete blank, she was staring into space wondering what to do next when a message boomed out over the public address system: **'*WOULD HOLLY AND EDWIN GOODCHILD PLEASE COLLECT THEIR TICKETS TO STRAWBRIDGE FROM THE TICKET OFFICE.*'**

Holly shook Edwin awake. 'Wha...wha...what...? he exclaimed, all sleepy-eyed.

'Ed, you'll never believe it but there are tickets waiting for us. Come on, we'd better get over there quickly, there might be a train leaving any minute.' Bounding to her feet, Holly was about to race over to the ticket office when she stopped dead. Who had bought them tickets? Could it be the witches? Except why would the witches have gone to the trouble of buying tickets? Why hadn't they just pounced on them? It didn't make sense. And the biggest mystery was how anyone knew they were heading for Strawbridge when, apart from Edwin, she hadn't told a single person.

Holly looked all around, just to make sure there were no witches lurking.

'Come on, Ed,' she said. 'It doesn't look as if we have much choice. We'll just have to take a risk.'

The man in the ticket office beamed, handed over the tickets and wished them a good day.

The train was crowded. Holly and Edwin sat near a group of children on a party outing. They chatted away noisily until they got off three stops down the line leaving behind discarded food and drink. Holly and Edwin couldn't believe their luck. There was one banana, half a packet of cheese and onion crisps, a few boiled sweets, and an unopened carton of Ribena. As the two tucked in, Edwin said it was better than Christmas.

When they reached Strawbridge, the ticket collector seemed more interested in eating a pork pie than taking their tickets

'Now what do we do?'

'I'm not sure,' Holly said. 'We've got to find Cherry Tree Cottage. Remember, it's right next door to the Cherry Tree pub so it shouldn't be that hard to find.'

'Why don't we ask someone?'

'Don't be silly,' Holly said. 'People will wonder why we don't know where we are. Next thing we'll be back scrubbing floors at the Holding Bay. We've got to work out ourselves how to get to there.'

'But s'posing when we get there, Uncle Tom and Aunt Bridget aren't there? S'posing they're on holiday?'

'They never go on holiday,' Holly said.

'S'posing they're out shopping?'

'We'll wait till they get back.'

'What if they're dead?'

'Don't be daft. Why would they be dead.'

'S'posing Mum is dead?' Edwin started snuffling.

'She isn't. Now come on.'

No sooner had they set off than an old van pulled up alongside them. The sight of their uncle behind the wheel was something Holly and Edwin would never forget for the rest of their lives.

Tom Goodchild was the spitting image of his brother, Jack. A big man with rosy cheeks, flaming red hair, the same colour as Holly's, trailed past his ears. Leaping out of his van, he looked ready to explode.

'What in tarnation are you doing here? We had a phone call telling us to pick you up at the station.'

Holly gasped. 'Who phoned you? Was it a witch?'

'A witch? No, it wasn't a witch. Well, not a female witch, at any rate. It was a man's voice, but I'm darned if I know who it was. Wouldn't give his name. But what are you doing here? Your mum didn't let us know you were coming.'

'That's 'cos Mum's gone off somewhere. When we got home from school, she'd vanished and these two men from the Ministry of CAWS forced us to go with them to the Holding Bay.'

Uncle Tom's jaw dropped a mile. 'But Alice would never just go off and leave you.'

'Well, I'm not making it up.'

'No, no of course you're not, Holly. But what about Jack? Where's your father?'

'He's working in Iceland,' Edwin piped up. 'And we haven't heard from him.'

Uncle Tom shook his head. 'Of all the places. Always was a god-damn fool,' he muttered. 'What a shock he'll get when he hears Alice has disappeared and you've turned up here.'

'We didn't run away from home, Uncle Tom. We ran away from the most horrible place in the world.' Holly told him about the two men from CAWS and the Holding Bay that was run by the witches and Red Vipereen.

Uncle Tom looked puzzled. 'Well, that's a new one on me. Ministry of CAWS, you say? And witches...well, I don't think they could have been witches, Holly.'

'They were, 'Holly insisted. 'Loads of them and they have these Harley Davidsons that can fly.' For the first time in her life, Holly felt close to tears. Edwin was already crying. 'Please, Uncle Tom,' Holly continued, 'don't let them take us back to the Holding Bay. I overheard Red Vipereen telling one of the witches to watch us day and night. Something weird is going on, and Red Vipereen is the weirdest looking thing I've ever seen. He said that now he had hold of Edwin, he could go ahead with his plans. Everything's weird. Look, who paid for our rail tickets to get to Strawbridge? And who was it phoned you?'

'So many questions!' Uncle Tom threw his giant arms round the pair of them. 'Don't worry your heads. Everything's going to be all right. Let's get you home and Aunt Bridget will know what to do.'

Sure enough, Aunt Bridget did know what to do. First, she made no end of phone calls. 'No-one's ever heard of the CAWS Ministry,' she said. 'And no one seems to have heard of a Holding Bay.'

'But we were there,' Holly insisted.

'Yes, we were,' Edwin echoed. 'There were lots of witches as well.'

'Something very strange is going on, that's for sure.' Aunt Bridget said. 'I can't find out anything about your mother's whereabouts, or where exactly your father is in Iceland. I've notified the police and that's about all I can do, for now. We'll just have to get on and do the best we can until we get further news.'

A great mountain of a woman, with saucer eyes, three chins and enough energy to launch a rocket, Aunt Bridget transformed their lives within days. Holly and Edwin decided their aunt's and uncle's thatched cottage was heaven. Even though the rooms were small and the ceilings low, it was cosy. There was carpeting wall-to-wall and knick-knacks everywhere. There was always plenty to eat – roast dinners some days and for tea, as many sandwiches as you could eat. Aunt Bridget didn't have to eke out everything as Mum had had to. For the first time the children had their own bedroom with thick, fluffy duvets and down-filled pillows. At night they lay in their beds as snug as anything and if the wind blew or the rain battered, nothing found a way in.

'We may not be rich,' Bridget Goodchild was forever saying, 'but I doubt there's anyone can make a pound stretch further than I can.'

It was all to do with her talent for haggling, Holly and Edwin soon discovered. Anything with a price and Aunt Bridget would put up a fight. 'Wimbally, wombally,' she'd cry before charging into battle. Now what wimbally, wombally, meant the children had no idea. But whether it was fish from the market or having the chimney swept, or buying plants for the garden, Bridget was ready to argue the toss. She also interested Holly and Edwin in everything she did. Holly loved baking cakes and working in the garden, but Edwin got tired very soon, whatever he did.

'You're not in the best of health, Edwin,' Aunt Bridget observed.

'He has asthma,' Holly said. 'He needs looking after.'

Bridget nodded. 'Yes, your mum was always saying that.'

Uncle Tom worked at Heal's shoe and slipper factory in the mornings. (The day after Holly and Edwin arrived, he presented them with new shoes and slippers.) He spent most afternoons tending his allotment and collecting up the eggs his chickens had laid. Sunday, however, was always a very special day. I(t was the one day of the week Tom set aside for painting.

One Sunday he invited Holly and Edwin to go with him.

My, aren't the two of you privileged,' Bridget exclaimed. 'Tom's never been known to take anyone with him before.'

Holly and Edwin helped their uncle load up his van with his painting equipment, plus a picnic hamper specially prepared by Bridget.

Tom drove deep into the country, pulling up by a lake with horses grazing in an adjacent meadow. In no time at all, he had everything set up, ready to start painting.

'It may surprise you to know,' he mumbled, a paintbrush clenched between his teeth as he unscrewed the top of a tube of paint, 'but I've sold quite a few horse paintings over the last few years. Not bad is that, seeing as I'm a self-taught artist.'

Edwin watched, mesmerised, as the horses came to life on canvas. 'They're fantastic,' Edwin said. 'I've only ever seen a horse on the telly. That brown one is the same colour as a conker. And that grey one with black spots is brilliant. Wish I could have a ride on one. Can I climb over the fence Uncle Tom and have a go?'

Uncle Tom shook his head. 'Certainly not. You could end up with a broken leg. We don't know how the horses would react. Besides, it's private property. The owners wouldn't want you trespassing.'

Edwin's face fell.

Holly wandered off to sit by the lake and watch the ducks gliding across the water. She was just thinking how lovely and peaceful it was when she heard Uncle Tom started shouting. 'Holly, Holly, come, quick.'

Holly ran back to find Uncle Tom hanging over the fence. 'Would you believe it,' her uncle whispered. 'I was so carried away with my painting I didn't see what the little rascal was up to. Look at that.'

There was Edwin stroking and talking to the chestnut horse who was loving every minute of it judging by all the head shaking and whinnying going on. It was as if

Edwin had been around horses all his life. And then to cap it all, the horse sort of half knelt so that Edwin could mount him. Holly held her breath. Edwin had never seen a horse before as far as she knew, let alone ridden one. But there he was scrambling up onto the big horse's back, no saddle or anything, and no sooner was the horse upright than they were off trotting around the meadow at a gentle, even pace, Edwin lightly holding the horse's mane.

'Can you believe it?' Uncle Tom laughed. 'Can you believe it?' he repeated. 'The boy's a natural and no mistake.'

Enjoying himself so much, Edwin was reluctant to join his uncle and sister for the picnic. While Holly and Uncle Tom tucked into beef sandwiches and lemon drizzle cake, enjoying every mouthful, Edwin sat eating like a robot, his eyes glued to the horses.

'Horatio's a lovely horse, isn't he?' Edwin said.

'How d'you know he's called Horatio?' Holly said.

'*He* told me. He also told me that he once belonged to a family who lived just down the road, but they didn't treat him very well.'

'Oh, yes.' Tom laughed. 'You're as good as your father at making up stories.'

'But I'm not making it up,' Edwin insisted. 'I could sort of pick up what he was thinking.'

Uncle Tom shook his head in disbelief. 'Well, I never,' he said. 'Whatever next?'

'I wish I could have riding lessons,' Edwin said on the drive home.

'Looks like you don't need any,' Uncle Tom said. 'You're a born rider, young man and don't worry, your time will come, you can be sure of it. Now before we go home there's something I think you should definitely see.'

Tom drove into the centre of Strawbridge, took a left, then a right and stopped outside a green gate in the middle of a high brick wall that ran in between two tall office blocks.

'Through that gate is Prince Rupert's palace and stables,' he said, his voice hushed. 'No one has ever been seen to go through the gate. And no one knows who, apart from the prince, is inside. But it's a well-known fact that Prince Rupert has a string of the finest horses in the world.'

Edwin's eyes were on stalks. 'It doesn't look much,' he said. 'The gate, I mean.'

'You couldn't squeeze a palace in between these buildings?' Holly said scornfully.

'Make no mistake, there's a palace and there are stables. And very special stables they are too. Every time the prince enters a horse in a race anywhere in the world, no other horse gets a look in.'

'Can we go inside?' Edwin begged.

''Fraid not, young man.'

'Where does the prince come from?' Holly said.

'From some island off the coast of Africa, is what I heard,' Tom said. 'I haven't seen him myself, but by all accounts, he is a handsome man, very striking. Rumour has it, and I don't know how much truth there is in it, mind, that thirteen years ago, the prince was visiting

England to buy a few horses for his stables back home – I'm not sure where that was. Anyway, while he was here, he met and fell in love with a beautiful young girl. He married her and whisked her back to his country, but she became very ill after giving birth to a baby girl and begged the prince to bring her back here to die. The prince did as she wished and then couldn't bring himself to leave the place where she was buried. So, he stayed and built himself a palace and stables right here.'

'I don't see why we can't see if the gate's open,' Holly said. 'Why don't we knock and see what happens?'

Uncle Tom gave a low whistle. 'We couldn't do a thing like that. It would be disrespectful.'

'Why?'

'It's common knowledge that no one gets inside. You'd stand a better chance of getting into Fort Knox.'

'What's Fort Knox?' Holly asked.

'A fortified building in America where lots of gold is stored.'

'Why have you brought us here, then?' Holly said crossly. 'Looks like we'll never get in.'

But that's where, for once, Holly was wrong.

A Royal Invitation

One evening, as Aunt Bridget was describing the school she had in mind for Holly and Edwin starting in September, there was a knock at the door. The couple rarely had visitors, so this was odd for a start.

'It must be someone from the pub next door,' Aunt Bridget said. 'Drunk as a skunk and wanting directions or a room for the night. Go and see them off the premises, Tom.'

It crossed Holly's mind that it might be the witches, but curiosity overcoming fear, she followed Uncle Tom into the hallway.

On the doorstep was a messenger boy in a bright pillar-box red uniform. The creases in his trousers were so sharp you could have peeled potatoes with them, and his narrow chest was so puffed up with pride, the brass buttons on his jacket were in danger of popping off.

He was holding out a gold salver on which was a gold envelope.

'I think you must have the wrong house,' Uncle Tom said gruffly and made to shut the door.

'Mr Tom Goodchild of Cherry Tree cottage?'

'Go on, Uncle Tom, open it.' Holly had to stop herself from grabbing the envelope. 'It's definitely for you. Let's see what's inside. Maybe you've come up on the lottery.'

Uncle Tom's hands trembled as he took the envelope. He opened it very carefully and took out a letter on gold paper.

He took so long reading it, Holly couldn't stand it.

'What does it say?' she begged. But Uncle Tom was in a kind of stupor. Holly snatched the letter from him and read it aloud:

The Palace and Stables
Strawbridge

Dear Mr Goody,

It has been brought to my attention that you have a fine reputation for painting horses. You sound just the man I am looking for and I would like to commission you to paint one of my horses.

If you are interested, I will make all the necessary arrangements for transporting you and your equipment to the palace. You will be able to set your own hours of work. Meals will be provided and, as well as paying whatever sum you stipulate for the painting, I will be happy to meet any out-of-pocket expenses.

My messenger will return tomorrow morning for your reply.

Yours very sincerely

(A squiggly signature)

'Who's it from?' Holly fixed the messenger with one of her looks.

'Prince Rupert, of course.'

Uncle Tom staggered back a few paces and Holly reached out to stop him falling.

'Yes, yes,' he stammered, trying to regain his composure. 'Yes, tell Prince Rupert I'll let him have an answer tomorrow morning.'

'Well. that's a bit daft,' Holly said. 'Why don't you accept now, Uncle Tom? You may never get another chance like this.'

'Yes, but well, there are things to be thought about, arrangements to be made?'

'What things?' Holly demanded.

'Yes, what arrangements?' Bridget echoed, coming up behind them. 'It's not every day you get an invitation from royalty.'

'But there's my job at Heal's to think of,' Uncle Tom protested. 'Not to mention the allotment. I can't just drop everything.'

'Stuff and nonsense,' Aunt Bridget said. She peered at the letter Holly was holding. 'It says clear enough, the prince will pay you anything you want.'

'You could be rich, Uncle Tom,' Holly exclaimed. 'Just think.'

'Maybe I could have riding lessons,' Edwin chimed in.

'You could have your own horse,' Holly said.

'Well...' Uncle Tom began.

Aunt Bridget smiled at the messenger. 'There's no need for you to return tomorrow morning. Tell the

Prince, Tom Goodchild is willing to paint his horse and start work as soon as possible.'

The boy nodded. 'If you'll be ready at midnight tonight, Mr Goodchild, someone will be along to collect you. There's no need to bring anything with you apart from your paints and brushes. Everything else will be provided for you.' This said, the messenger gave a smart salute, walked quickly down the garden path, mounted a small red motorbike and sped off.

Somehow, Holly and Edwin crawled through the rest of the day. Although they usually went to bed around 7 p.m. Aunt Bridget said that as it was a very special occasion, they could stay up to see Uncle Tom off.

Sure enough, on the stroke of midnight, there was a ratatat on the front door.

'Well, go on, Tom, what are you waiting for?' Bridget gave her husband a shove.

A broad-shouldered chauffeur, with a handlebar moustache and bulbous nose, stood outside. Behind him, under a streetlamp, was a silver-grey stretch limousine, exactly the same colour as the chauffeur's uniform.

The chauffeur clicked his heels together. 'Evening, sir, Charles Reilly at your service. Luggage, sir?'

Uncle Tom was so flustered, his wife had to come to the rescue. 'We were told Tom wouldn't need anything apart from his painting stuff which we've got all ready and waiting.'

'That is indeed the case, Madame,' the chauffeur said. 'Allow me, Madame,' he reached out and took a cardboard box full of paints and brushes together with an easel. He smiled at Uncle Tom. 'If you would follow me, sir.'

All four of them followed the chauffeur out to the stretch limo, which was even bigger and swankier than the Ministry of CAWS Rolls and watched as Charles Reilly carefully placed the box and easel in the boot.

When the chauffeur swept open the car door, Uncle Tom scrambled inside in a rather undignified manner. Aunt Bridget and the children were so stunned by everything, they forgot to wave goodbye. They just stood in the lane gawping as the beautiful limo glided silently off into the distance.

After a drink of cocoa, Aunt Bridget packed the children off to bed and went straight to bed herself. Try as they might, the children couldn't get to sleep. Edwin crept into Holly's room.

'Hey sis, are you awake?'

'I am now,' Holly said, although she hadn't been able to sleep either.

Edwin climbed onto Holly's bed and sat cross-legged. What do you think Uncle Tom's doing now?'

'Sleeping, I should think.'

'Yes, but where? What sort of a bed will he be in?'

'How should I know, but I bet it's a very scrumptious bed.'

'What does scrumptious mean?'

Holly didn't think 'scrumptious' was the right word, but she couldn't tell Edwin that. 'It means very rich.'

'I wish I could see the horses in the prince's stables.'

'You never know we might get to see them, seeing as we now have royal connections.'

'We might get a Christmas card from the prince.'

'And birthday cards.'

Aunt Bridget came storming in. 'Back to your own room, Edwin Goodchild,' she ordered. 'Some people round here would like to get a wink of sleep if you don't mind.'

The children did finally get to sleep. Awake at the crack of dawn, Holly heard her aunt bustling about downstairs. And over the following days, while Uncle Tom was away, Holly noticed that her aunt was more bustly than usual. She spring-cleaned the house from top to bottom and insisted on taking the children shopping to buy school uniforms.

Holly was the first to spot the stretch limo drawing up outside. All three rushed outside to greet Uncle Tom and there were tears in Tom Goodchild's eyes as he embraced each of them in turn.

Pulling her uncle into the house, Holly almost pushed him into his favourite armchair.

'Now tell us everything that happened,' she said, when they were all sitting down. 'Every bit of detail. Don't leave anything out.'

But Uncle Tom was shaking his head. 'I'm very sorry,' he said. 'But I can't remember. I can't remember a blessed thing.'

'What?' the three chorused, in dismay.

'Before I left, they gave me this sweet to suck. It was like one of those old-fashioned humbugs. Anyway, after sucking it, I couldn't remember anything that happened. I remember going there and coming back. But the bit in between, well, it's gone, I'm afraid. I've racked my brains for some fragment or other, but nothing's coming back.'

'But what about the painting you did? You must remember that,' Holly said. 'Did you finish it?'

'I must have.'

'You must have seen the prince and the horses.'

'I must have, but I can't remember.'

'Did you get paid for your work?' Aunt Bridget cut in.

Uncle Tom felt in all his pockets. 'It doesn't look like it.'

'Oh, Tom,' his wife cried. 'Why didn't you think to ask? What a cheek that prince has got, taking advantage of you like that.'

In the early hours of the morning, when everyone was fast asleep, Holly was woken up by a loud crack of thunder. A storm was raging outside, a wind so strong she thought the thatched roof would blow off. One extra big whoosh and one of the windowpanes shattered, scattering glass all over the floor. When she looked out of the broken window, to her horror, Holly saw the Holding Bay witches flying round and round the house on their motorbikes, Red Vipereen, with his long beard and glowing red eyes, at the helm. The witches looked like they were sniffing the air for all they were worth.

The noise of breaking glass brought Edwin hurrying into the room, closely followed by Uncle Tom and Aunt Bridget.

Edwin was crying. 'I hate storms.' Aunt Bridget wrapped her arms around him.

'Goodness, I've never known a storm so fierce. Look at that. It's gone and broken the window. Wimbally, wombally, whatever next.'

'It's the witches and Red Vipereen,' Holly said. 'I bet they magicked up the storm. Look out of the window if you don't believe me.'

Both Uncle Tom and Aunt Bridget rushed over to the window.

'There's nothing,' Uncle Tom said. 'Nothing at all, only the branches of the trees doing a merry dance in the wind.'

'Well, there were witches. Honestly. You think I dreamt it, don't you? Well, I didn't. You've got to believe me,' Holly said. 'I really did see them flying round the house on their motorbikes.'

'There's definitely something peculiar going on.' Uncle Tom looked pale and anxious.

Edwin started crying. 'They'll catch us and take us back to that horrible dump.'

'Not if I have anything to do with it,' Uncle Tom said. 'Now then, all three of you get some blankets and get yourselves down to the cellar. You'll be safer there than anywhere.'

Uncle Tom grabbed hold of a lethal-looking shillelagh and swung it round his head, with surprising ferocity. 'Any witches try to invade my home they'll wish they'd never been born.'

The sun was shining radiantly the next morning, everything back to normal, and if it hadn't been for the broken glass all over the living room floor, Holly might well have thought she **had** dreamt the whole thing about Red Vipereen and his flying witches. But as Uncle Tom was about to leave the house to go to Heal's factory, there was a loud knock on the front door.

'The witches!' Uncle Tom bellowed, his red cheeks turning white as chalk. Edwin and Aunt Bridget immediately raced for the cellar while Uncle Tom picked up his shillelagh and with Holly close behind, made his way to the front door.

A Visit to the Prince's Stables

On the doorstep was a man with raven black hair, swept straight back off a high brow, rich, dark chocolate skin and molten brown eyes. The man was immaculately dressed in a cream suit, mustard coloured shirt and red bow tie. Looking past the very handsome man, Holly saw the silver-grey, stretch limo with Charles Reilly at the wheel.

'Prince Rupert,' Uncle Tom said in hushed tones. 'I know that's who you are, although how I know, I've no idea.'

'Mr Goodchild,' the prince flashed a brilliant white smile. 'I wanted to pay you a personal visit to let you know how delighted I am with your painting.' He glanced down at the shillelagh Uncle Tom was still clutching.

Tom gave a weak smile. 'Sorry, you can't be too careful these days.' He propped the weapon by the side of the door. 'Well, I'm glad you liked the painting. But you know, I can't for the life of me remember what it was like.'

'Ah yes, the forget sweet,' the prince nodded. 'A very necessary precaution, I'm afraid. We have some special secrets to preserve, you see. Now then, you are a fine artist, Mr Goodchild. Please name your fee so I can settle up at once.'

'Well, er...' Uncle Tom looked around for help. 'Oh, er... this is my niece.'

The prince smiled. 'Good morning, Holly.'

Uncle Tom looked taken aback. 'You know her name.'

'You told us all about Holly and Edwin.'

'Well, I'm blowed. Maybe I told you what a rough time they've had as well, their father going off to Iceland and their mother disappearing. If there's one thing the two of them would like more than anything it would be to see your stables.'

'That's more or less what you told us, Mr Goodchild,' the prince said.

Holly pushed past her uncle and stuck out a hand. 'How-do-you-do, Prince Rupert.'

'Delighted to meet you,' the prince said, warmly shaking her hand. 'Is your brother around?'

'Yes, he is,' Holly said. 'He's in the cellar.'

'The cellar!' The prince looked shocked.

'Because of the storm last night,' Uncle Tom said quickly. 'And well Holly thought she... er...saw...er...' Uncle Tom's voice trailed off.

'Storm. I didn't know there was a storm last night.' The prince turned and gazed up at the sun-filled blue sky.

'I'm s...sorry,' Uncle Tom stammered. 'Look, I don't know what we're doing keeping you standing on the step. Come inside, please.'

Uncle Tom led the way into the living room. 'The storm was so fierce the children were scared. To be honest, Holly here thought she saw witches flying round the house. You know what children are?'

'I did see witches,' Holly butted in. 'And that's why you sent us down the cellar, Uncle Tom. You were scared as well. You stayed up all night with that spiky thing in case the witches tried to break in.'

Uncle Tom looked sheepish.

The prince, on the other hand, was clearly perturbed. 'Witches, you say?'

Uncle Tom nodded. 'That's why when you knocked at the door just now, Edwin thought the witches were back, so he took himself off to the cellar. My wife's down there with him.'

'Hang on and I'll go and get them,' Holly offered.

She called down the cellar steps. 'Edwin, Aunt Bridget, we've someone very important come to see us. It's the prince.'

And before you could say 'shillelagh' Aunt Bridget and Edwin were up the steps and bursting into the room.

The prince gave one of his dazzling smiles and shook each of them by the hand 'So very nice to meet you and I do apologise for whisking Mr Goodchild away so abruptly the other day.' He looked at the children, his expression very serious. 'So, you actually saw witches flying round the house.'

'They were the witches from the Holding Bay trying to recapture us,' Holly said. 'Red Vipereen was with them as well.'

The prince gasped. 'You've met Red Vipereen?'

'Sort of,' Holly said. 'I think I saw him once flying past our bedroom window back in Barford and I definitely saw him talking to a witch at the Holding Bay. And guess what, they were talking about us. The witch said she bet he was pleased to get his hands on us. She meant Ed and me.'

'Yes, yes, go on.' The prince dabbed at his noble brow with a blue silk handkerchief.

Holly thought for a moment. 'Oh yes, he said something about the other lot hadn't got Wizard Grindsniff to help them.'

The prince shook his head. 'Ah, Wizard Grindsniff. That was a sad business. Very sad. To this day, we don't know for sure what happened to him. But thank you, Holly, for that information. And now, I must return immediately to the palace and consult Madame Fosse. She's our resident psychic. I always consult Madame Fosse on any important matters, and she's never let me down so far, although, of late...' his voice trailed off.

'But who is Wizard Grindsniff?' Holly said. 'And what has Red Vipereen got to do with you and what...?'

The prince held up his hand. 'Please, I'm afraid I can't go into any details at the moment.' He looked at Uncle Tom. 'I would be delighted to have Holly and Edwin visit the stables, Mr Goodchild. I shall make arrangements at once, if that's all right with you. But please, let me know what your fee is for that wonderful painting.'

Tom looked embarrassed. 'Well, really, I don't know. I mean...'

'The saints preserve us,' Bridget cut in. 'My husband has no head on him for business, Prince Rupert. Would £1000 be asking too much?'

'Not at all,' the prince smiled and produced an envelope which he handed to Tom. 'I hope you will find that sufficient, Mr Goodchild to cover the cost of the painting and any expenses,'

The minute the prince had gone, Aunt Bridget threw up her hands. 'Well, don't just stand there, Tom, open the envelope and put us out of our misery.'

Everyone waited impatiently while Tom slowly opened the envelope and drew out a cheque. 'Well?' Bridget said.

Tom looked too shocked to speak. He handed the cheque to his wife.

'Wimbally, Wombally,' Bridget exclaimed. 'Five thousand pounds. Five thousand pounds for your painting, Tom. And there I was thinking one thousand was a lot of money. Makes you wonder whether Prince Rupert has more money than sense.'

'He said he'd make arrangements for us to visit his stables,' Edwin said.

'Yes, well I shouldn't bank on that if I were you,' Bridget said.

Tom shook his head. 'I'm sure he'll keep his word. He's a man of integrity, you can see.'

'We'll have to wait and see what happens,' Holly said.

Fortunately, they didn't have to wait long. In less than two hours the messenger was at the door with a letter.

The Palace and Stables
Strawbridge

Dear Mr and Mrs Goodchild,

On behalf of Prince Rupert, I would like to invite Holly and Edwin to stay with us from tomorrow until they go back to school in September. If you are agreeable, Charles Reilly will call round for your niece and nephew at 5 p.m. There is no need for them to bring anything as everything will be provided.

Apologies for such short notice.

Yours truly,

Mr Mistoses
Secretary-in-Residence

Having agreed on the spot to her husband being whisked off to paint a horse, Aunt Bridget now came up with a million and one reasons why Holly and Edwin shouldn't go.

'We've no knowledge of what goes on there,' she said. 'And you not remembering a thing of what went on doesn't help any, Tom. And what if the children come back not even remembering they've been born? I don't like it one bit. Wimbally, wombally, I don't like it at all. Haven't the children been through enough without adding to their troubles. For all we know, we might never see the two of them again.'

'But...' Uncle Tom tried to stop the flow.

'Holly and Edwin are your own flesh and blood, Tom. They're like the children we never had and if we send them off to this palace place, we could be endangering their lives.'

'But...'

'And here's Edwin with his asthma. He needs to take things easy, not get mixed up with wizards and witches.'

'Prince Rupert has been very generous,' Tom reminded her.

'Too generous, in my opinion,' Bridget said. 'Who's to say this isn't some kind of bribe and we never see the children again.'

Edwin burst into tears and Uncle Tom looked so miserable, Holly thought he might start crying as well.

Aunt Bridget appeared to have won the day. When the limousine arrived the next day, she said she would send the chauffeur packing.

Holly thought and thought and eventually came up with an idea. She whispered to her brother. 'Edwin, listen. This is what we're going to do.'

Thinking she would give the children a special treat, Aunt Bridget made their favourite meal of beef stew and dumplings and couldn't believe it when the children sat straight backed in their chairs, arms folded, and refused to eat a morsel. They sat in silence, staring straight ahead of them. Holly had warned Edwin not to look at the food or even smell it, or he might be tempted.

'What's the matter with the pair of you,' Aunt Bridget demanded. 'What do you think you're playing at?'

Holly and Edwin remained silent.

'Oh, I see, this is punishment is it for not getting your own way? Now let me tell you something. The pair of you aren't old enough to know what's best for you.'

Holly bit her tongue.

'Oh well, it doesn't matter to me whether you eat or not. The food's there and, for afters, there's ice cream as a special treat. But please yourselves.'

In bed, Holly's stomach rumbled like thunder. Halfway through the night, Edwin crept into her bedroom.

'I can't sleep, I'm so hungry,' he said.

'And I'm not, I suppose,' Holly snapped. 'Do you want to see the horses or not?'

Edwin nodded. 'More than anything in the world.'

'Well then, get back to bed. And remember, no breakfast in the morning, even if you think you're going to faint.'

When the children gave a repeat performance at breakfast time, Aunt Bridget couldn't stand it any longer. She rang Dr Crick and demanded that he see Holly and Edwin immediately because they were about to die of starvation. Dr Crick said he couldn't waste his time on visits of no importance and that the children would eat when they couldn't hold out any longer. Aunt Bridget fumed and cursed the doctor, said that Dr Crick should be renamed Dr Thick. And she told Holly and Edwin that they were driving her to an early grave.

At 4.55p.m. five minutes before Charles Reilly was due to arrive, Aunt Bridget gave in.

'All right, all right,' she cried in frustration. 'You win. Maybe it'll be all right. Your uncle came back unharmed.

So, all right, the two of you can go. If for no other reason than to get some food inside you.'

Holly immediately flung her arms round her aunt and kissed her while Edwin made funny whooping noises at the back of his throat.

Charles Reilly arrived at 5 o'clock on the dot. Still full of apprehension, tears streamed down Aunt Bridget's face as she hugged the children to her. 'You'll take good care of them, won't you?' she begged.

'You need have no fear, ma'am,' Charles said. 'They'll be in safe hands.'

'Good luck,' Uncle Tom called as the children climbed into the car. His red cheeks were glowing like beacons and there was a happy smile on his face as he wiped away a tear.

A Royal Reception

Forgetting no one could see in through the tinted windows, Holly pretended she was the prince's daughter and waved to passers-by in what she hoped was a regal manner.

When they reached the green gate, Charles sprang out of the car, held open the door and wished them good luck. 'All you have to do is knock on the gate twice. Someone is waiting the other side.'

Holly and Edwin were walking towards the gate when they heard an all too familiar roaring sound. In the sky was a dark cloud of witches. As the cloud came nearer and nearer, the noise got louder and louder. Edwin was glued to the spot, so Holly had to grab hold of him and drag him towards the entrance. She banged on the gate twice and, as if by magic, it opened instantly. Inside, they found themselves in a courtyard.

In the centre was a large shed in front of which stood a tubby little man with a beachball body, beachball head, spindly arms and legs, and ears and fingers studded with rings. Completely bald, the man wore a tight-fitting bodysuit and green trainers.

The dark cloud overhead had disappeared. Instead, the witches were hurling themselves at the gate. Wasting no time, the strange little man threw open the shed door to reveal a large platform with a pole in the middle.

'Mr Mistoses, at your service,' the man said in a high squeaky voice. He leapt high into the air and kicked his legs sideways. 'Please, please, this way. Don't worry, you're quite safe. No witch has ever yet got through that gate.'

Mr Mistoses pointed to the platform. 'Please, please nothing to worry about. It's only a lift to take us down to the palace stables.'

Cautiously, Holly approached the lift, Edwin creeping behind her.

'But it's got no sides,' Holly exclaimed. 'We could fall off.'

'Please, please. Nothing to worry about,' Mistoses repeated. 'Just keep a firm hold on the pole and you'll come to no harm.'

'Come on, Edwin,' Holly urged her brother. 'You want to see the horses, don't you?'

No sooner had the three of them stepped onto the platform and grasped the pole than they started moving, slowly at first, then, as the lift gathered momentum, they went streaking down a deep, dark shaft at an alarming rate. They were going so fast, Holly wondered if the lift was out of control and whether Edwin's heart was thumping as hard as hers. If it was, she just hoped he wouldn't have another of his asthma attacks or do something stupid.

Miles below the surface of the earth, the lift slowed before coming to a halt. Mr Mistoses stepped out and led the way to a brightly coloured vehicle that looked a bit like a tramcar. Inside, the seats were as big and ornate as thrones. The floor was spread with rugs, the windows hung with silk drapes. The minute they were seated, Mr Mistoses pressed a button and off they zoomed through a long dark tunnel, going so fast that Edwin turned white, and Holly closed her eyes.

'We've arrived,' Mr Mistoses sang out. 'Please alight.'

Opening her eyes, Holly was dazzled by brightness. They were in a quadrangle with stables ranged around the sides and light pouring down from a domed glass roof.

Mr Mistoses bounced out of the train and did another funny leap in the air. 'Welcome to Prince Rupert's palace and stables.'

Instantly recovering from his fright, Edwin hurtled across the yard to stand on tiptoe and peer first into one stable, and then another.

'But there aren't any horses.'

'Out for a spot of training with Schlox their trainer, I expect,' Mr Mistoses said. 'Don't worry. They'll be back soon.'

Taking a look for herself, Holly discovered all the stables were light, airy and spotless, each one bearing a name on a gold plaque – Fury, Arthur, Conan, Hector, Ercol, Gaul, Ulysses, Grey of Maccha, Moriah, Nessa, Diarmud and Black of Saingland. Six grooms were hard at work making up beds of hay and replenishing water containers. All the grooms were exactly alike with large heads, bowlegs, bright, tiny eyes and large noses with a wart on the left side.

Holly looked over at Mistoses. 'They're all…'

'…the same,' Mistoses supplied. 'That's because they are. Identical sextuplets. 'And guess what? They all live up to their family motto. "*Happy is the man who works. Sad for life, he who shirks.*" Come along, I'll introduce you. Unfortunately, Trotter, the Head Groom's not here at the moment but you'll get to meet him soon enough.'

Each groom gave the same cheery grin and shook hands in exactly the same way. Mistoses reeled off their names – Grobbly, Snobbley, Wobbley, Cobbley, Bobbley and Hobbley.

Holly was puzzling as to how Mistoses could tell one from the other when the horses, eyes shining and covered in sweat, together with the jockeys, filed back into the yard. Leading the procession was a thin, wiry man with cropped, blond hair and ice-blue eyes behind wire-framed spectacles.

'Here come the jockeys with the horses. And here comes Schlox, their trainer,' Mistoses said. 'What fine horses. Indeed. Indeed.' And he burst into song and made another of his spectacular leaps.

Scratchamanoses and ticklematoeses
Oh, everything's roses
For Mr Mistoses

The jockeys bowed or doffed their hats in Holly and Edwin's direction before taking themselves off leaving the grooms to get to work sponging and brushing the horses. Mistoses introduced Holly and Edwin to Schlox.

The trainer gave a stiff bow.

'Best trainer there is,' Mistoses said, watching Schlox disappear in the same direction as the jockeys. 'Doesn't say much but gets on well with the horses and that's what counts.'

'Good looking bunch, aren't they?' A voice from behind Holly and Edwin had them spinning round. Prince Rupert, dressed in a long flowing green and yellow silk robe, looked taller and more regal than they remembered.

'Will we be able to help with the horses?' Edwin said.

'You'll do better than that, you'll learn to ride them.'

'Wow.' Edwin jumped up and down with excitement.

'But you're not to go overdoing it,' Holly warned. 'He's got asthma,' she explained.

'Don't worry, we'll take good care of your brother,' the prince reassured. 'If he feels at all unwell, I have a very good resident physician.' He paused for a moment. 'Is there anything else worrying either of you?'

'Lots,' Holly said. 'We nearly didn't get here, 'cos the witches were chasing us. And I keep wondering why you let us come here? I know Uncle Tom did that painting for you, but he said no one from outside has ever been allowed in?'

'I'm going to be totally honest with you, Holly,' Prince Rupert said. 'Madame Fosse, our resident psychic, learned about the two of you a short while ago. With the help of her Diviner, she predicts that Edwin is going to be helpful to us in a forthcoming crisis, although what that crisis will be and when it will occur, she doesn't know.'

'My brother? Are you joking?'

'Me...?' Edwin squeaked. 'Must be another Edwin.'

The prince shook his head. 'Madame Fosse rarely makes mistakes. For some time now we've been having problems and we suspect that Red Vipereen, a thoroughly evil wizard, is behind everything.'

Holly nodded. 'I told you, we saw him at the Holding Bay. What kind of problems has he caused?'

'Oh, so many. First, there was a plague of mice, then beetles. Then we had the entire palace filled with the stench of rotten eggs. Not long after that, a mysterious fire broke out in the west wing. Our treasured palace cat was found drowned. For no reason, people have been falling down the palace stairs. And, just recently, Madame Fosse, herself, was unable to get out of bed. She reckons there's more to come.'

Holly's head was teeming with questions, but where to begin. 'Was it you who bought the train tickets for us?'

'With the help of her Diviner, Madame Fosse detected that you were in trouble and er...yes, we were able to arrange that at short notice. '

'And does Madame Fosse know about the witches at the Holding Bay? And what about Red Vipereen? Remember, I told you I overheard...'

The prince held up his hand. 'Please. I wish I could tell you more, but Madame Fosse has been having a few problems with her Diviner of late and the messages coming through are none too clear. We just have to be patient. And now if you'll excuse me, I have much to do.'

Once the horses were settled in their stalls, Mistoses introduced Holly and Edwin to each of them in turn. Some whinnied and pawed the ground, others shook their heads. 'They're well looked after,' Edwin said. 'They love it here. I can tell,' he said.

'You don't know that for sure.' Holly threw out.

'Oh, but I do,' Edwin said. 'They've just told me.'

'Come off it, Edwin,' Holly said. 'Don't make things up. You're getting to be like Dad.'

'I'm not making it up. I'm not.' Edwin insisted.

Mistoses squawked. 'Would you believe it. Would you believe it. The boy can tell what they're thinking. Well, I never.'

Edwin spent some extra time stroking Fury, a deep russet coloured horse with a white star on his forehead. Holly was more drawn to Grey of Maccha, a very graceful grey mare who looked deep and wistfully into Holly's eyes.

'Come, come,' Mistoses urged. 'I've saved the best till last. You've yet to meet a very special horse. He led the way to the very end stable. 'Take a look. See what you think. This is Black of Saingland,' Mistoses said, almost in a whisper.

Raven black, with eyes to match, the horse gave them a condescending stare. Dark and mysterious, he was extremely handsome, but there was also something a bit scary about him.

'This is the prince's horse,' Mistoses continued. 'The horse your uncle painted. He is by far the most talented horse in the stables. A genius and no mistake. Can you imagine a horse that can race as fast as the wind? Jump as high as a house? Pivot like a ballerina? Well, Black here can. His father was Coeur De Lyon and his mother was the famous Blue Tango.'

Edwin studied Black for a while, then leaned towards him and whispered in his ear.

'I suppose *he's* told you something as well,' Holly taunted.

Edwin nodded. 'He says he's being trained for the Mission, whatever that is.'

Mistoses looked stunned. 'Did he now? Did he?'

'So, what's the Mission?' Holly asked.

Mistoses shook his head. 'Ah, now. You'll have to ask Prince Rupert about that. All I can say is that unless the Mission goes ahead, we're all in mortal danger.'

A Feast Fit for a Horse

As if worried he'd said too much already, Mistoses abruptly changed the subject. 'I must show you to your rooms. You must prepare for this evening. Come, follow me.'

A grand staircase and a labyrinth of corridors led to a high-ceilinged, marble-floored bedroom with tall windows overlooking the palace grounds. There were two four-poster beds hung with rich velvet drapes. 'One for each of you,' Mistoses explained. 'And, as you can see, clothes for this evening have been laid out.'

Holly ran over to the bed and scooping up a beautiful green silk dress she held it against her and danced around the room. 'Look, it's just the right size. Oh, won't I look great in this,' she exclaimed. For Edwin there was a red, velvet suit, white shirt and black bow tie.

'You also have a bathroom,' Mistoses continued. 'I think you'll already find the baths have been run for you. You'll find towels, soap, toothbrushes, everything you need to hand. Now I'll leave you to it. If there's anything else you need, you only have to ring the bell by the side of the bed.'

'When you hear the gong make your way to the banqueting hall which is down the stairs and off to the right. Prince Rupert doesn't like to be kept waiting. He's very easy-going in most respects, but he's a stickler about timekeeping. Also, there's one rule above all others that must be strictly adhered to. You must not go wandering around the palace or outside, after ten p.m. You'll see notices posted everywhere to this effect.'

When Mr Mistoses had gone, Holly spun around the large room, inspected the marble-tiled bathrooms, and threw herself on the bed where she lay spread-eagled. 'Have you ever seen anything like this, Edwin?'

''Course I haven't,' Edwin said. 'I bet Uncle Tom had a great time, except he can't remember any of it. D'you think we'll be made to forget we were here as well, sis?'

'Right now, I'm not bothered one way or the other. And you shouldn't be either. We should make the most of it, 'cos we may never have anything like this again. But come on, we must get ready and not be late for the meal.'

Timed to perfection, the gong sounded the minute they were ready and dressed. Back down the staircase they tripped and into a magnificent banqueting hall where over a hundred people were gathered. In the centre of the room was a huge round table, sparkling with silver. Light from an outsize chandelier bounced off walls hung with tapestries and lit up shoals of exotic fish swimming in a glass centrepiece on the table.

'We must be the last. Now we're for it, we're late.' The words were no sooner out of Holly's mouth than everyone in the room rose to their feet, turned towards them and bowed.

Holly and Edwin froze on the spot as all eyes centred on them and everyone started clapping. Prince Rupert came towards them, arms outstretched, a huge welcoming smile on his face.

'Holly and Edwin, honoured guests, it is my very great pleasure to formally welcome you to the palace. I trust your stay with us will be hugely enjoyable.

'First, let me introduce you to my daughter, Cate.'

Cate, about the same age as Holly, had the same black hair and dark skin of her father but her eyes were a kind of violet shade. When she gave a wide, open smile, Holly knew straight off they would get on well.

'And this is Madame Fosse, our resident psychic.' A fierce-looking woman with dark, hooded eyes gave the special guests a haughty stare and a curt nod. The psychic, draped in black lace from head to foot was drenched in jewellery that jingle-jangled when she gave them a wave.

'And that will do for the moment,' the prince said. No use introducing you to everyone. Far too confusing.'

It was a long time since Holly and Edwin had eaten so when huge bowls of something that looked like a cross between seaweed and spaghetti arrived on the table, they were extremely disappointed. Edwin's face was every bit as glum as the grooms sitting opposite. He craned to see what was in another bowl further along the table.

'It's all the same,' Cate told him.

'It looks yuk,' Edwin said.

'Oh, but it isn't,' Cate said. 'It's brilliant and every bit is grown in the palace grounds by Mulch, the head gardener. What you have to do is heap some on your plate then close your eyes and think of your favourite food. You'll be surprised.'

Holly helped herself to a few scoops of the purplish stuff and hooking some onto her fork followed Cate's instructions. Concentrating as hard as she could she imagined the Sunday roast beef and Yorkshire pudding at Cherry Tree cottage. Expecting to taste something disgusting, instead she savoured all the mouth-watering flavours of her favourite meal.

'Wowee,' Edwin shouted. 'Chocolate pudding and ice-cream. It works.'

Prince Rupert was smiling broadly. 'Help yourselves to as much as you want. And why not imagine a few other dishes.'

Edwin wasn't interested in anything else. He had another helping of chocolate pudding and ice-cream. Holly's apple pie and custard had never tasted so delicious.

'You can do the same with the water,' Cate said, pouring each of them a glass.

Holly closed her eyes and sipped. 'Mmm. Strawberries,' she murmured.

'Great,' Edwin gulped down a few mouthfuls. 'Lemonade.'

'The horses have the same food,' Prince Rupert said. 'It has magic properties that help horses and people maximise their full potential in the shortest possible time. Of course, some will always be more talented than others, but whatever is there, this food will bring out the best.'

For all that she was enjoying the experience, Holly could not help but be aware of the silent, brooding presence of Madame Fosse beside her. So, when the psychic spoke to her for the first time, she nearly jumped a mile. A deep, bell voice rang out. 'Do you expect to see your mother and father again?'

'Of course,' Holly said, a bit too brightly. 'But we don't know where they are. Would your Diviner be able to tell us?'

A vigorous shake of the psychic's head sparked a merry tune. 'My predictions are solely concerned with the safety of the palace.' She paused. 'Now, I should very much like you to tell me about the witches.'

Holly told what she knew, which wasn't a lot, but even so, she was aware that everyone around her, including the prince and Cate, was hanging on her every word.

'And what do you know about Vipereen?' Madame Fosse demanded.

'Not much.'

'I'd still like to hear.'

Holly repeated the brief conversation between Vipereen and the witch, following which Madame Fosse flounced back in her chair with much jangling.

'Red Vipereen is really scary,' Holly said.'

Madame Fosse nodded. 'Indeed he is, Holly. And he is becoming more powerful within the palace with each passing day. But how he is managing to do that I have no idea. Someone inside the palace must be helping him and whoever it is, must be stopped. Unfortunately, we no longer have Wizard Grindsniff to call on for assistance.'

'Prince Rupert told us a bit about Wizard Grindsniff. But what does Red Vipereen want? Why did he want to get hold of Edwin and me?'

There was no reply. Madame Fosse was in a deep, deep trance.

Riding Lessons

Edwin's whooping and yelling brought Holly out of a troubled sleep. 'Wowee. Yahoo. Crikey. Look at this. We're going riding.'

Holly rubbed her eyes. 'Er...what...? What...?'

'Look,' Edwin held up a pair of jodhpurs and a riding hat. 'We must be going riding today.'

Sitting up, Holly discovered a complete riding outfit at the foot of her bed: cream jodhpurs, black jacket and riding hat, gloves and by the side of the bed a pair of black leather riding boots. 'When did all this stuff arrive?' she asked.

'Someone must have brought it in the night.' Edwin donned the hat and pulled on the riding jacket over his pyjama top.

'Must have been fairies,' Holly said, preparing to go back to sleep.

'Oh, come on, sis. I can't wait.'

Holly thought of the horses. How big they were. It was all right for Edwin. Seemed like he had a knack with horses, even knew what they were thinking or so he said. Supposing she fell off? Everyone would laugh.

Going down to breakfast, dressed in the riding gear, Holly's legs were trembling.

Watching Edwin gobbling down his seaweed, Holly didn't feel up to eating. And all too soon, Mr Mistoses appeared, ready to escort them to the stables. Trotter, the head groom, a thin, horsy faced man invited them to choose a horse. Without hesitation, Edwin picked Fury and Holly went for Grey of Maccha.

'Good, good. Very good in fact.' Mistoses enthused. 'Upon my soul, wonderful,' he said, executing his famous leap. 'And here comes your trainer, Schlox. Bang on time. Good morning, Schlox. Your pupils are as eager as can be.'

Holly groaned.

Schlox gave the pupils a steely appraisal. 'One of your jacket buttons is undone, Edwin,' he snapped. 'Now, has either of you had riding lessons before?'

'No, we haven't.' Holly forced herself to look into Schlox' cold eyes. 'I haven't ever been on a horse, but Edwin has. He hasn't had an actual lesson, but my uncle said he was a natural.'

Schlox gave a thin-lipped smile. 'That remains to be seen.'

As Fury and Grey of Maccha were being tacked up, Holly couldn't stop gazing up at the horses. Up close, they were ginormous.

'Watch your step with Fury, Edwin,' Mistoses warned. 'He's inclined to live up to his name. A real paddy on him at times. Take control and show him who's boss.'

Ready to put up a fight, Fury stamped the ground and snorted. Far from being afraid, *Edwin, The Terrified,* reached out and began gently stroking the angry horse. Quietening down, Fury pulled back his upper lip and gave a high-pitched whinny.

'Would you believe it,' Mistoses gurgled. 'He's smiling, Edwin. He's actually smiling.'

Holly wasn't used to her brother receiving all the praise. Plucking up courage, she reached towards Grey of Maccha intending to stroke her neck but stepped back quickly when Grey brought her large head close to hers.

'Nothing to be alarmed about,' Mistoses reassured. 'She wants to give you a friendly nuzzle. Grey is a very sweet, gentle horse. Not a malicious bone in her body.'

'Enough of this nonsense,' Schlox barked. 'We haven't got all day. If you don't mind, perhaps we can make our way to the paddock.'

Edwin insisted on leading Fury, but Holly was quite happy to let Grey be led by one of the grooms.

To reach the paddock, the horses were led along a narrow, sloping path that ran between tiered lawns with bright flower beds in the centre, the flowers forming the shape of horses. Busy tending the beds was an army of tiny gardeners no bigger than three feet tall.

'Cor, look at those titchy men,' Edwin cried.

'Don't be rude,' Holly snapped.

'Indeed, they are small,' Mistoses agreed. 'Smaller than me, in fact, but how useful being so close to the ground, don't you think? They all have an amazing sense of smell as well. Some are better than hunting dogs, would you believe. But uh-oh, watch your step Edwin, Mulch, the head gardener, has got his beady eye on us.'

A bird flew overhead. Mistoses waved. The bird squawked in return. 'That's Rory,' Mistoses said. 'The falcon was Wizard Grindsniff's constant companion. Such a pity Grindsniff is no longer with us.'

Rory flew down, landed on Mistoses' shoulder where he sat throwing foul looks at Holly and Edwin. The falcon was so unnerving that Holly was relieved when it took to the skies again.

'Cor, wizards and falcons.' Edwin was so intent on staring up at the falcon that he accidentally stepped onto the lawn, taking Fury with him.

Mulch, a thick-set grumpy-looking man, began shouting and waving his arms. 'Oy, keep them bloomin' creatures off me gardens, will ya! Can't yer read?' He pointed to a notice: HORSES MUST STICK TO THE PATH.

Edwin stepped smartly back onto the path, but not before Fury had sunk his hooves into the pristine lawn.

'If I 'ad a gun on me, I'd shoot the bloomin' lot o' yer,' Mulch shouted.

'Sorry,' Edwin called.

'Oh, just ignore old Mulch,' Mistoses said cheerfully. 'I don't know why the prince employs him. He hates horses. Only has time for his plants.'

'Gerrof wi' yer,' Mulch shouted again.

Holly fought to hold her tongue. After all, she and Edwin were guests.

'Never gets out of bed the right side,' Mistoses muttered.

Mulch had to be the rudest man she'd ever met, Holly decided.

On reaching the paddock, they found two young boys leaning against the rail.

'Hi, I'm Liam Trotter,' one of them said. 'My dad's the head groom. You've probably met him.' Liam was a sturdy boy with thick, straight brown hair and a habit of flicking a forelock out of his eyes.

The other boy looked shy. He had lots more freckles than Holly and his hair was more sandy than carroty. 'Oh, er...I'm Sean Ainsley. My dad's the blacksmith.'

'How long have you two been riding?' Liam asked.

'This will be our first lesson,' Holly said.

Liam laughed scornfully. 'I've been riding for ages. Since I was two. I can do loads of things.'

Holly and Edwin glanced at each other. Neither of them was very impressed with Liam. Schlox and Mistoses had been joined by two men, both very tall and thin. One had a thick mane of white-gold hair and a pointed chin. The other was nearly bald and seemed to be talking to himself and giggling.

'Who are they?' Holly asked.

'The one on the right, next to Schlox is Phelps, the vet,' Sean said. 'He also looks after us if we're ill.'

'What, we see a vet!' Holly couldn't believe her ears. 'But what if my brother...'

She stopped herself. Edwin's asthma was none of Liam's business.

'What about your brother?' Liam demanded. 'Something wrong with him?'

'No. Nothing.' Holly dug Edwin in the ribs to stop him saying anything.

'We call Phelps, the Leper,' Sean said. "'Cos nobody wants to go near him. In case they get foot and mouth or something.'

Edwin giggled.

'Who's the other man?' Holly said. 'He looks a bit mad.'

'He is mad,' Liam said. 'He's the horse shrink. His name's Longbottom, but we call him Bonkers.'

Bonkers was still jabbering away to himself.

'What exactly is a horse shrink?'

Both Liam and Sean laughed.

'Like a psychiatrist,' Liam said.

'But Bonkers is really good with horses,' Sean said. 'He always knows what's bothering them.'

'We've got names for everyone,' Liam said. 'Schlox is the Fox, 'cos he's sly.

'I reckon he's more scary than sly,' Holly said.

'And Mistoses is Squishy-Squashy,' Liam went on. Madame Fosse is Madame Cross, and the palace librarian is Snooze, 'cos he's always sleeping.'

'No one knows what Snooze's real name is,' Sean said. 'Even Prince Rupert calls him Snooze.'

It was getting weirder by the minute, Holly thought, but she didn't say anything.

Schlox was now signalling for Holly and Edwin to join him inside the paddock.

Holly was hugely relieved when Phelps, The Leper, rounded up Liam and Sean and, together with Bonkers, they headed back to the palace. The idea of being made a laughingstock in front of Liam would have been more than she could bear. She didn't mind Mistoses staying. Better than being left alone with Schlox.

'To begin with, you'll be led around on a leading rein,' the trainer barked. 'Get you used to the horses. Now then, up you get the two of you.' He nodded towards the mounting blocks that had been placed beside the horses. Edwin didn't need asking twice. In the blink of an eye, he was up on Fury's back. Holly had to be helped by one of the grooms.

As the grooms tightened everything up, Holly looked down and gulped. The ground was a long way off. Schlox told her to keep her head up. The trainer had no problem with Edwin who hadn't stopped smiling. It was a different matter with Holly.

'Holly, stop slouching. Stop looking at the ground. Shoulders back. Head up.'

Schlox was a tyrant, Holly decided. A martin... something or other and no mistake.

Finally, they were ready and while Schlox stood in the middle of the yard, two of the grooms led them around in a circle.

Half an hour later, the pupils were instructed how to hold the reins. Edwin was perfectly at ease, but Holly wasn't at all comfortable being in charge of Grey. Out the corner of her eye, she could see Mr Mistoses nodding approval and winking.

When Schlox tried to move them on to do a 'sitting trot'. Holly was in danger of losing her nerve. Trying as hard as she could to keep her seat, she lost track of Edwin, so that when he came trotting past her at a lick, she fell off her horse in astonishment. Bruised and shaken, she managed to get herself back in the saddle with the help of a groom. Schlox, his eyes fixed on Edwin, appeared to have lost interest in her. Holly took several, deep, steadying breaths. How was it that her brother, useless at everything, was finding this riding business a doddle? And how long was this torture going to last?

Here came Edwin, overtaking her again. And not only was he looking as relaxed as anything, he was actually talking to Fury.

'Good boy, Fury. What a great horse you are. The best.'

Sick making.

And again, he sailed past. 'Atta boy. Fury. Having a great time, aren't we.' As if he'd been speaking to horses for years. And there was Fury, ears pricked, looking for all the world as if he were carrying the world's No. 1 rider on his back.

Smelly.

Mr Mistoses was beside himself, leaping repeatedly and warbling:

Oh, fabulosis and wonderfalosis
Mr Mistoses
Is smelling of roses

The lesson over, Holly discovered she could barely stand. How she made it back to the stables, she didn't know. But Edwin, fresh as a lemon, insisted on helping to untack Fury while Holly slumped against a stable door. Mistoses squatted down beside her. 'Would you believe it,' he muttered. 'Boy's a natural like his uncle said. He's got the horse gene for certain. And he's got the hands, you can tell. Magic hands. The voice to go with them as well. Upon my word, I've never seen anything like it. Such a pity old Grindsniff isn't here to see it.'

Holly would have liked to hear more about Grindsniff, but she was too tired to ask. She limped behind her brother as they made their way through the palace. They hadn't gone far when they bumped into some of the palace children, including Cate, clustered round a notice board outside the palace library. A Notice read:

ANYONE UNDER THE AGE OF 14 YEARS WHO WANTS TO TAKE PART IN THE SHERGAR OBSTACLE RACE ON FRIDAY, 3 AUGUST SHOULD WRITE THEIR NAME BELOW

Cate explained. 'It's an annual event specially for us.'

Holly realised everyone was looking at them.

'Don't suppose you've got to know anyone yet?' Cate said.

'They know Sean and me.' Liam sniggered. 'We saw them having their first riding lesson.'

'What's so funny about that,' Cate snapped.

'And you didn't see us having a lesson,' Holly retorted. 'You left before we got started.'

'How many times did you fall off?' Liam persisted.

'You're pathetic, Liam Trotter,' Cate said, and went on to introduce the others. Petunia, small and pretty was ten, Patrick, tall and lanky with glasses was Holly's age,

Mary-Jane, plump and cheery, was eleven, Wendy, with pigtails and a big gap between her front teeth, was also eleven and Graeme, with big round eyes in a round face, was twelve.

'What's Shergar?' Edwin asked.

Liam sneered. 'Don't tell me you've never heard of Shergar, the famous racehorse. You must be the only one in the world who's never heard of him.'

Holly rushed to her brother's defence. 'There must be loads who haven't heard of him. So there.'

'You know what? You're as stupid as your brother,' Liam jeered.

'Oh, you're just a big bully, Liam,' Cate said and went on to explain that Shergar was stolen a long time ago and added, 'And to this day, no-one knows what happened to him.'

Edwin looked at Cate. 'Could I enter the race?'

'Don't be daft,' Holly cut in. 'You've only had one lesson, Ed. And it's an obstacle race. You'd have to be jumping over things and stuff.'

'It's not all that difficult,' Mary-Jane said.

'Go on, I dare you, 'Liam goaded. 'Leave carrot top behind, Eddie. Go on, put your name down.'

'Who are you calling carrot top?' Holly demanded.

Liam pretended to look all around. 'Er…er…anyone seen any other ginger nuts about?'

Patrick, who was much taller than Liam, the tallest in the class, in fact, pushed his specs up his nose and shoved his way to the front of the group. 'Leave off calling Holly names, Liam Trotter,' he threatened, 'or you'll get what's coming to you.'

A scowling Liam poked Patrick in the chest. 'Mind your own business, spotty, squirty four eyes,' he said and pushed past to add his name with a great flourish.

'If I put my name down, will you, sis?' Edwin asked.

Liam gave a horrible laugh. 'Weedy weed can't do anything on his own.'

'Yes, I can,' Edwin said, squaring his narrow shoulders.

Holly took a deep breath. 'You know what, Liam Trotter, we're both going to enter the race, aren't we Edwin? How about that?'

Liam opened his mouth to say something, but Holly shot him such a deadly look, he quickly closed it again. And, not giving herself time to think, Holly added her name and waited for Edwin to do the same.

'The only thing is, I'm not so sure the race will go ahead,' Cate said. 'Some of the horses have gone down with some kind of bug. They were all fine yesterday. Now about three or four are really sick. The Leper is just hoping the rest don't go down with whatever it is.'

Holly was secretly hoping the race wouldn't be able to go ahead, but she could see how concerned Cate was.

'What's the cause?' she asked.

Cate shrugged. 'They've never had anything like this before. But, as you may have heard, Holly, there have been lots of strange things happening in the palace of late. If you see anything suspicious, anything suspicious at all, you must let my father know at once.'

Secrets at Midnight

H olly lay awake worrying about the Shergar Obstacle Race. How stupid she'd been to put her name down just to spite Liam Trotter. Edwin was brilliant with horses, so maybe he'd be all right, but she was barely able to stay on a horse let alone deal with obstacles. Cate had said some of the horses were sick so there was a chance the race might be cancelled. On the other hand, if she got herself along to the notice board, she could scrub her name off the list

It was close on midnight when Holly left her bedroom. She knew quite well that if she was caught, Prince Rupert would be furious. Everywhere you looked there were notices:

ANY UNAUTHORISED PERSON FOUND WANDERING AROUND THE PALACE OR THE PALACE GROUNDS AFTER 10PM WILL BE INSTANTLY DISMISSED FROM THE PREMISES.

Unsure of the layout, Holly set off down the corridor. Everywhere was pitch black. All she could do was pray she was going in the right direction. After turning right at the end of the corridor, she turned sharp left and right and again and down a flight of stairs. From memory, Holly judged the library and notice board were straight ahead, but as she made her way along the dark passageway, she heard footsteps.

Holly made it to the library, felt for the handle and found the door unlocked. Throwing open the door she flung herself inside and closed the door as quietly as she could behind her.

Night lighters helped her make out a shape slumped over a desk in the far corner. It had to be Snooze, the palace librarian.

The footsteps stopped outside the library. Any minute now and someone would enter the room and discover her. With no time to lose, Holly pulled open the doors to a large cupboard, crawled inside and pulled the doors shut.

'We can talk in here. A brass band wouldn't wake Snooze.'

Holly recognised Schlox's icy tone.

'Come on, come on, then. Spit it out. What exactly are ya accusin' me of this time?'

Holly instantly recognised the gruff voice of Mulch, the head gardener.

'Everyone knows you've no time for the horses,' Schlox said.

'What's the point yer makin'?' Mulch sounded ugly, but not half as menacing as Schlox.

'The point is, I believe the food has been tampered with.'

'Food's same as what we all eat. So don't come any o' that malarkey.'

'We're probably not affected in the same way as the horses. Or maybe it's just taking longer with us.'

'Now listen, you keep on accusing me o' any of this bloomin' stuff and I'll knock ya inta next week. Get it? My job is overseeing my staff. I don't go messin' with no plants that's turned into food. Right?'

'Easy enough for you to get one of the gardeners to do your dirty work or...'

Holly heard the door open followed by Madame Fosse's booming voice. 'What's going on in here? Schlox. Mulch. What are you up to?'

'If you don't mind, we're trying to have a private conversation' Schlox said.

'At midnight? You know perfectly well prince Rupert forbids anyone wandering around after curfew.'

'And what d'you think you're doing then?'

'The prince has given me special permission.'

'What's so special about you?' Schlox snarled.

'How dare you?' This followed by a loud jangling.

'Aw right, aw right, don't get your knickers in a twist,' Mulch snapped. 'I've no particular wish anyways to carry on this conversation. You go right ahead, Schlox, speak direct with the prince.'

'What are you talking about?' Madame Fosse demanded. 'What allegations? What's going on?'

'Schlox is accusin' me of poisonin' the horses, that's what,' Mulch growled.

'Oh, get out of my way, the pair of you,' Schlox snapped and stomped out of the room.

Holly waited until all the footsteps had died away before leaving her hiding place. Making sure the coast was clear, she made her way over to the notice board only to find the Shergar Obstacle Race list had been removed. All her risk-taking had been for nothing. But what about the conversation she'd overheard? Mistoses had said how Mulch hated the horses. What if he hated them enough to poison them?

A Thief in the Night

Holly had no sooner returned to her room than a storm broke out. Normally, she wasn't in the least bit scared of storms, but this one had her all on edge. What if she'd been caught breaking the ten o'clock curfew? She decided she wouldn't tell her brother, or anyone else for that matter, what she'd been up to. If Liam got to hear she'd tried to wriggle out of the race, she'd never hear the last of it.

Listening to the howling wind and claps of thunder, Holly's head buzzed with questions. Why had Mum suddenly disappeared? Why hadn't they heard from Dad? Had Aunt Bridget and Uncle Tom seen anything more of the witches and Red Vipereen? How come Edwin had such a superpower with horses? And why had Edwin been singled out to help the palace? Another thought struck her. The storm outside? She could hear the rain lashing down. Snuggling down under the duvet, she wondered whether it was a real storm. Or was it the witches trying to get in? What was all that about Mulch poisoning the horses? And what was she going to do about the obstacle race?

The next morning, still groggy from lack of sleep, Holly followed Edwin down to breakfast only to find another shock waiting.

The usually quiet great hall was a hubbub of noise and commotion. Prince Rupert was standing in the centre whilst a swarm of palace staff with horror-stricken faces zoomed this way and that, getting nowhere fast. Next to Prince Rupert, Madame Fosse was seated at a small table frantically rubbing the screen of her Diviner. Mr Mistoses was pacing up and down and wringing his hands.

Holly went over to him. 'What's happened?'

'Simply dreadful.' Mistoses clasped his hands together. 'Black of Saingland, our beloved Mission horse, has been stolen. Disappeared. Vanished into thin air. Oh, doom and gloom. What's to become of us:

> *Oh calamitous, calamity*
> *Hubbly and bubbly,*
> *It's doubly troubly.*

The palace secretary continued wailing, 'Oh hubbly, bubbly, doubly troubly,' and went whizzing off to join the mad swirl.

Cate, a doleful look on her usually happy face, came over, 'It was Madame Fosse   who discovered Black had been stolen. When she felt a storm coming on, she got up and went for a walk. That's when she found the men guarding Black all fast asleep. Someone must have drugged them or hypnotised them, or something.

We think Black was stolen when they were dead to the world.'

'I bet Red Vipereen stole him,' Edwin burst out.

'I bet he did,' Cate said. 'Or someone is helping him. Mulch and all his gardeners are out searching the grounds. Trotter has taken to his bed because of it all and my father's so upset, he can't think straight. Without Black, The Mission can't go ahead, and the palace is in deadly danger.'

A Cry for Help

Wendy pulled a long face. 'Don't expect there'll be any riding today.' Her brace made the words come out all muffled.

'Don't expect there'll be much of anything.' Patrick said, his long face as glum as a rainy day. 'What with Black going missing and some of the horses sick, next thing the Shergar race'll be cancelled.'

If only, Holly thought. And what about the conversation she'd overheard between Mulch and Schlox? Should she tell Prince Rupert, even if it meant admitting she'd be wandering round the palace at midnight? If Mulch was behind poisoning the horses, he had to be the one helping Red Vipereen. Was it Mulch who'd stolen Black? On the other hand, if the horses had picked up some bug, she didn't want to go dropping Mulch in it. Besides, Madame Fosse knew as much as she did about Schlox accusing Mulch of tampering with the food. It was up to her to tell the prince.

'Does anyone know yet what's making the horses sick?' Holly asked.

Cate shook her head. 'So many strange things keep happening.'

'The Leper thinks it's something the horses have eaten,' Patrick said.

'Yes, but they have the same food as us, don't they?' Holly said.

There was a sudden silence as they all stared at one another.

'So, we might all get sick,' Wendy blurted out.

'Except sick's nothing compared to Black being stolen,' Cate said.

'D'you think Black's dead?' Edwin's voice trembled.

'No one knows,' Cate said. 'Even Madame Fosse doesn't know what's...' A scream interrupted her.

Madame Fosse, her face drained of colour, had stopped rubbing her Diviner and was staring at it transfixed. Everyone crowded round, pushing and shoving to get as close as they could to Madame Fosse and the prince. Holly and Edwin, somewhere in the middle of the scrum, couldn't see a thing, but they heard Madame Fosse say 'I have received two messages. First, *that a search party must be formed.*'

The words spun round and round the great hall like a top.

A search party must be formed. A Search Party Must Be Formed. A SEARCH PARTY MUST BE FORMED. ***A SEARCH PARTY MUST BE FORMED.***

The words got louder and louder until the sound was so ear-splitting a massive gong was sounded to quieten everyone. Holly was wondering what the second message was when the sea of people parted, and Prince Rupert came walking towards them. He gave a small bow in front of Edwin. 'Madame Fosse says we need to launch a search beyond the palace grounds to find Black of Saingland and that you, Edwin, must lead the search.'

'Wha...what...meee?' came out as a strangled squawk, followed by a frantic, pleading look at Holly.

Prince Rupert turned to Holly. 'Of course, you must come too, my dear.'

'But, if you don't really need me,' Holly retorted. 'I'm not going anywhere I'm not wanted.'

'I can't go without my sister. I can't lead a search party,' Edwin shrieked.

Prince Rupert gave a deep bow. 'Please, I beg you both. Help us. Maybe it would be useful if I explained... Perhaps I should explain. Please, come with me. We need to speak in private.'

The prince and Madame Fosse led the way to the library where a matted grey head and beard lay across a desk. Snooze was woken up and sent scuttling out of the room. The four of them then sat themselves down at one of the library tables and tried to ignore Snooze weeping and wailing out in the corridor.

Prince Rupert set about explaining the dire consequences of losing Black of Saingland.

He nodded towards an oil painting over the marble fireplace. 'That is your uncle's painting of Black.'

'Cor, that's great,' Edwin said. 'Uncle Tom's a brilliant artist, isn't he?'

'Indeed. A great painting of a great horse. You see, Black is the only horse capable of undertaking The Mission. For some time now, the palace has been under threat from the Powers of Darkness over which Red Vipereen has complete control. Red Vipereen's burning ambition is to gain control of the palace and, especially the stables. Vipereen has a passion for horses and, for many years, has been envious of the palace's reputation. With Wizard Grindsniff's assistance, we were able to keep Vipereen at bay, but ever since the palace wizard disappeared three years ago, we've had nothing but trouble.

'We've advertised for a Powers of Darkness Adversary, someone to replace Wizard Grindsniff. We've advertised many times, in fact. It doesn't have to be a wizard, so long as it's someone with enough power to counteract Red Vipereen. But finding the right calibre of person is proving difficult, if not impossible.

'Some time ago, I came to the conclusion that the only way to guarantee the safety of the palace was to lay claim to the Blessed Crystal, a magical crystal that has the power to give us complete protection from evil. However, gaining possession of the crystal involves a long and hazardous mission. Black was the only horse capable of undertaking such a hazardous journey.'

He broke off, overcome with emotion. From the depths of her voluminous black robes, Madame Fosse produced a hip flask from which the prince took a few grateful sips.

'For two years,' the prince continued, 'we have been planning an expedition to claim the Blessed Crystal, but until Black of Saingland came along we could never find a horse with the stamina and bravery for such a strenuous journey.'

Once again, catching sight of Tom Goody's painting of Black of Saingland, the Prince welled up. He took another few sips from the flask.

'Black had almost finished his training. Through the Diviner, Madame Fosse has learned that Black is to be found somewhere in the Grindsniff Wastelands, an expanse of land beyond the palace boundaries.'

'Grindsniff was a very loyal and wonderful palace wizard. I will not hear a word said against him. Not long after we opened the stables, Mistoses advertised for a wizard, and we were immensely lucky to have Grindsniff apply. Since his disappearance…or more likely his death, three years ago, we've been at a complete loss.

'Unfortunately, our wizard was a little on the conceited side and he had a rather over-curious nature. Not content with being a famous wizard, he wanted to be a famous explorer as well. So, one day, two years ago, almost to the day, without a word to anyone, he set off on his own to explore the wastelands, a wild and unexplored area of land beyond the palace boundaries. He was gone a long time and we all feared for his safety, particularly as we'd heard rumours that Red Vipereen had laid claim to the wastelands. Sadly, we still have no knowledge of what happened to dear old Grindsniff, except that, before whatever befell him, he sent back a map of the area with Rory, the falcon, his only companion on the trip. The wizard named the land after himself. To date, no-one has ventured into that dark territory.

'It appears we must now do so, and Madame Fosse tells me that you're the one, Edwin, who can help us find Black.'

Edwin gulped. 'But...'

'Oh indeed, yes,' Madame Fosse said briskly. 'My Diviner shows you as being extremely instrumental in the search.'

Edwin looked terrified. 'But...but...I won't be able to do it on my own.'

'Of course not,' Prince Rupert said. 'I will accompany you. Holly will come too. Also, I propose that Mr Mistoses, a very able rider and a completely trustworthy...'

Holly broke in. 'What do you mean? You don't mean we're supposed to go searching for Black on horseback?'

The prince smiled. 'That was the general idea.'

'But we can't ride. I mean, well, I can't...I've only been on...'

'You will have training. Seven days in fact. Madame Fosse forecasts the most auspicious day to begin the search is seven days from now.'

'Seven days,' Holly exploded. 'But that's nothing. That's only a week.'

'You will have Schlox to train you. He is one of the finest trainers there is. And I can promise you that if at any point our lives are in danger, we will turn back,' the prince said. 'I give you my solemn word on that.'

'And what about the horses?' Holly was getting desperate. 'I thought lots of them were sick?'

The prince nodded. 'Indeed, it is a worrying situation. We've quarantined those who are sick and are closely guarding the others. We can only hope the ones who are ill make a speedy recovery and that none of the others is affected.

'How Red Vipereen has infiltrated the palace is a mystery. Many years ago, Grindsniff cast a PSS over the palace making it impossible for any outside wizards or witches to penetrate the building or grounds.'

'What's a PSS?' Edwin asked.

'A Permanent Seal Spell. Very powerful. Unbreakable. Or so we thought.'

Not giving herself time to think, Holly blurted out. 'Maybe Mulch is poisoning the horses. He grows all the food. Maybe he's working with Red Vipereen.' She stared at Madame Fosse, willing her to back her up.

Prince Rupert looked shocked. 'But Mulch has been with us for years,' he said. 'Oh, I know he is a curmudgeonly character and doesn't care for horses, but he has always been a loyal servant and I cannot believe he's in cahoots with Vipereen. Nevertheless,' he looked over at Madame Fosse. 'What do you think?'

Madame Fosse shook her dark head. 'I have no evidence to suggest Mulch is a traitor. No evidence at all.'

Holly bit her tongue and decided she'd said enough on the subject.

'And as I was saying,' the prince continued, 'about the training...'

'You seem to have forgotten that Edwin has asthma,' Holly interrupted. 'He's the last one to be doing anything dangerous.'

Madame Fosse and Prince Rupert looked as if they'd been flattened by a meteorite.

'But since I've been here, I haven't had a single attack,' Edwin said.

'We'll provide all the equipment needed for the trip,' the prince said. He paused. 'And you can make a wish, Edwin.' He looked at Holly. 'Both of you. Before you leave and, once we have Black safely back, I guarantee your wishes will be granted.'

Madame Fosse jingle jangled as she rocked back in her chair.

Holly and Edwin looked at each other. There were things they wished for more than anything else in the world.

'So, will you do it, Edwin? Holly? Prince Rupert said. 'This very noble deed? The palace would always be indebted to you.'

'All right,' Edwin said. 'I'll do it. I will help you find Black.'

'Oh, no,' Holly groaned. 'Look what happened to Wizard Grindsniff. Ended up dead, most likely. And he was clever. What chance do we stand?'

The Training Begins

Four days into a gruelling training programme, Edwin was taking everything in his stride and enjoying every minute. Holly was hating every second *and* having to work ten times as hard as her brother just to keep up. Covered in bruises and aching in every muscle she thought it more likely she'd end up in hospital rather than help in the search for Black. How was it her weedy brother was going from strength to strength? All she could do was look on in amazement as Edwin executed Flying Leaps, Kangaroo Walks, Highland Flings and Bronco Bucks. She honestly believed Fury would do a cartwheel if Edwin asked him to. It wasn't fair. To add to her misery, Holly was having to train on Nessa because Grey had also gone down sick.

Throughout the whole of their training, Holly and Edwin were kept separate from everyone else. Meals were taken in their bedroom, with palace guards posted outside and the same guards accompanying them everywhere they went. Red Vipereen was going to find it hard to get at them. And, as if the training wasn't enough, they were given loads of books to read: *Ancient and*

Modern History of Horses by Felix Gallops…*The Tibetan Book of Thoroughbred Training, Blood Horses Down the Ages, Horse Ancestry, Wild Horses of the Plains* and *The Equine Encyclopaedia…* Worn out at the end of each day, Holly usually fell asleep over a book, but Edwin, who'd never been much of a reader, read each one from cover to cover.

Now and then, on their way to a training session, they bumped into some of the other children.

'Lucky old you,' Wendy said.

Holly muttered something unprintable under her breath.

'You're real heroes,' Patrick said, pushing his glasses up his nose. 'Won't be long now before you're off. I'll miss you, Holly,' he added, turning bright red.

'You might be knighted or something,' Graeme said.

'We could end up dead,' Holly said.

Liam, of course, did nothing but jeer while Edwin reckoned Liam's face had gone permanently green with envy.

'Don't forget it's the Shergar obstacle race tomorrow,' Cate reminded them.

Holly stiffened. The obstacle race! She'd forgotten all about it.

Edwin's face was glowing. 'We wouldn't want to miss that, would we, sis?'

Holly could have strangled him. 'We won't be able to, Edwin,' she said sharply. 'I mean, Prince Rupert wouldn't want us to. I mean, supposing we had an accident. The search for Black would have to be called off.'

'Oh, I've already had a word with my father,' Cate said. 'And he says it's up to you. It's not as if the race is dangerous or anything.'

Holly frowned. 'But are the horses up to it?'

'Most of them are better, thank goodness,' Cate said.

'Oh, look,' Liam jeered. 'Holly's scared.

Holly lifted her head and used her emerald eyes to best effect. 'No, I'm not. You just wait and see, Liam Trotter.'

Liam gave another horrible laugh and walked away.

Obstacles Galore

On the morning of the Shergar Obstacle Race, Pinch and Pouch, two gardeners whose sense of smell was the most highly developed of all the gardeners, returned to the palace with the news that they'd picked up the scent of Black of Saingland on the edge of the Grindsniff Wastelands. It wasn't much to go on, but it was enough to lift spirits and dispel some of the gloom that had settled over the palace.

Having taken it upon himself to escort Holly and Edwin to the racecourse, Mr Mistoses led the way to the stable yard. A leap into the air and a clap of the palace secretary's hands and a large blue buggy appeared from nowhere. Mistoses handed Holly and Edwin a plan of the racecourse. 'Study it as we go,' he suggested, before taking the wheel.

Making sense of the plan wasn't easy, not when they were whizzing along at the speed of light, but from what she could make out, Holly didn't like the look of it one bit. One big obstacle after another from what she could make of it. If she had any sense, she told herself, she'd swallow her pride and withdraw from the race? What did it matter if Edwin was trembling with excitement?

'Can't wait, can *you* sis?' he said.

Holly muttered under her breath.

Zipping along, they sped past paddocks, circumnavigated a wood and several hills until they came to an entrance over which was a white banner with three-foot high black lettering:

THE SHERGAR OBSTACLE RACE

An impressive racecourse was overrun with palace gardeners scurrying over the emerald turf plucking out specks that were invisible to the naked eye.

Down one side of the course, flags and bunting fluttered from the stands. Prince Rupert was seated between Madame Fosse and Bonkers in the Royal Enclosure.

The weather was on its best behaviour, the sun shining brilliantly in a cloudless sky.

Mistoses hurried Holly and Edwin into the saddling enclosure where an impatient Schlox was striding up and down, looking as if he might snap in half at any moment.

'You're late,' he barked. 'What the devil are you about, cutting it so fine? I've a good mind to scratch the pair of you.'

'Hey, steady on. Hold your horses,' Mistoses chuckled. 'They'll be ready in two shakes of a horse's tail.'

Before Holly and Edwin could don the special riding silks all ready and waiting – yellow and purple for

Edwin, red and black for Holly, which clashed with her hair – they had to be checked over by the Leper in the Examination Room. Before he got to work with a stethoscope, Holly warned him: 'My brother has asthma.'

The Leper cocked his head to one side. 'Something going on, that's for sure, but I'm not sure what,' he announced. 'Are you up to this, young man?'

'Course, I am,' Edwin protested. 'And you'd better hurry up. Schlox is getting in a state.'

'You're sure Edwin be all right?' Holly asked, after her own brief examination.

'I hope so.' The Leper sounded doubtful. 'But to be on the safe side, you'd better take something, Edwin.'

The Leper filled a tumbler with something resembling orangeade to which he added half a teaspoon of yellow powder. 'Drink that down, my boy, and you should be as right as rain.'

After a mad scramble to get dressed in their silks and take a last look at the racecourse layout, Holly and Edwin went to collect their horses from the saddling enclosure, and that's when Holly discovered she was expected to ride Nessa, Grey of Maccha being still unwell. It wasn't as if there was anything wrong with Nessa who was a very handsome mare with a distinctive white stripe on her forehead, but it wasn't Grey.

'I can't ride Nessa,' Holly protested. 'I just can't.'

'Come along, you've wasted enough of my precious time,' snapped Schlox.

Petrified, Holly was ready to call it quits, but seeing Edwin astride Fury and looking supremely confident,

Holly gritted her teeth and let one of the grooms help her mount Nessa.

As they cantered up to the starting post, Holly risked a glance at the Royal Enclosure and saw that Schlox had now joined the group.

Liam, riding Ulysses, came up in between Edwin and Holly.

'Ulysses is the best horse in the race and I'm one of the best riders, so you don't stand a chance, Edwin,' he sneered. 'And even if you had the best horse, Holly, you'll end up last, that's if you even manage to finish.'

'We'll have to see, won't we,' Edwin shot back, not in the least bit fazed.

'You sure will.' Liam aimed a savage kick at Fury's flank. Fury reacted by rearing up so that Edwin had his work cut out keeping his seat. Holly held her breath, thinking the race might be over for Edwin before it had even got started.

Quickly, Edwin regained control. 'Good lad, Fury,' he murmured. 'Nothing to worry about. Only stupid old Liam trying to spook us. We're going to enjoy this race whether we win or not. Okay?'

Seven of them were soon lined up and under starter's orders. Petunia, the only one missing, had lost her nerve at the last minute. Holly wished with all her heart she'd followed Petunia's example.

Whilst Liam had placed himself in the centre of the line-up, Edwin had settled on the outside with Holly next to him. Cate in black and gold and riding Moriah, was the other side of Holly. She looked across and mouthed the words *good luck*.

Three false starts, with Liam to blame each time, had such an unsettling effect on the field that Holly reckoned he should have been disqualified. But finally, they were off with Patrick on Hector streaking out in front closely followed by Cate.

Holly was happy to settle at the back, tucked in behind Graeme. Out of harm's way, there was a chance of her keeping her seat; also, she had a clear view of the field and how things were going.

Liam and his friend, Sean, riding Conan, were starting to close on the leading pair. Edwin, holding his position on the outside was not in contention.

Coming up fast was the first obstacle, Over the Rainbow, a low, rainbow coloured bridge. The leaders sailed over the rainbow with ease; nor did Nessa find it difficult.

Already, Liam and Sean had overtaken Patrick and Cate, but Edwin was steadily gaining on them. Holly had no time to take in anything else because coming up was Dinosaur Alley. The first dinosaur lying sprawled across their path was a Tyrannosaurus rex; tail swishing, jaws opening and shutting, it was so life-like, Holly's heart skipped a beat. Nessa wasn't so easily fooled. Picking up speed, she took the obstacle in her stride.

Next, a Brontosaurus lay in wait. Lying on its back, dinosaur legs clawed the air. Holly surrendered control to Nessa who dealt swiftly and easily with the recumbent creature. Only one more dinosaur to go. Even though she was trailing the field, Holly was starting to enjoy herself. So long as she could go at her own pace and get over the obstacles in her own time, she didn't mind if she came last. A Stegosaurus loomed, its spiky scales pointing skyward, demanding respect. Holly closed her eyes as they soared upwards and only opened them again once they'd landed the other side. Patrick was now only a yard or so in front of her, his flying start having fallen away.

Holly had almost caught him up as they sped towards Castle Moat. Ahead of them, everyone sailed safely over. His body stretching and folding to the rhythm of Fury, Edwin had increased his gain on Liam and Sean. That was all Holly had time to take in, because Castle Moat was right ahead, crocodiles poking their ugly snouts out of the water. Of course, they weren't real crocodiles, Holly knew that, but they but they were scary all the same. The real threat was the water. Wide and probably deep. Nessa gathered speed and opened her shoulders. Up...up...And down, safely the other side.

'Well done, Nessa, that was...' Holly broke off, realising a dense fog was closing in on them. Apart from Graeme who, unseated, was picking himself up off the ground, the rest of the field had been swallowed up by the fog.

Losing all sense of direction and unable to see an inch in front of them, Holly felt Nessa's body tense as she applied the brakes and began rearing and plunging.

When the horse gave a high-pitched scream, Holly's fear quickly gave way to anger. Up to now the obstacles hadn't been difficult for the horses. But this was something else. What was Prince Rupert thinking about? Surely, he knew how dangerous fog was for horses?

Within minutes, however, as fast as the fog had descended, it cleared and not a minute too soon. Nessa was just in time to veer around Sean's prostrate body. Already people were racing over to the boy on the ground. Mistoses in the lead, was closely followed by Trotter, Schlox, Bonkers and The Leper.

Holly could now see Liam and Edwin racing neck and neck, closely followed by Cate. All three were heading for the final obstacle - Hoop-la. - a row of hoops big enough for the horses to sail through. Through the hoops and the leading three would be on the home straight.

Edwin and Liam were about to take the hoops together when, to Holly's horror, she saw the hoops burst into flames and begin whizzing round like Catherine wheels. Horses and riders were about to be eaten by the flames. Chaos broke out amongst the rest of the field. Cate's horse turned right around and came racing back towards Holly. Wendy's horse reared up, sending Wendy hurtling to the ground. Patrick had dismounted and was running for his life, holding his glasses in place as he ran.

Nessa, confused and terrified, was galloping blindly towards the blazing hoops. If she stopped abruptly, Holly expected to be flung into the fire. Not knowing what to do, Holly flung her arms round Nessa's neck and buried her head in the horse's mane. Nessa soared into the air. A fierce heat enveloped them. Holly thought her hair had caught fire. The next instant, Nessa's hooves thudded down. Miraculously, they had made it through.

Up ahead, Holly made out Mary-Jane, on Arthur no more than a few yards behind Edwin and Liam who were now racing toward the finishing post, Liam slightly in the lead.

Liam was whipping Ulysses over and over, trying to maintain his lead, but Edwin, crouched low, was catching up fast. When they were matching stride for stride. Liam's whip came up once more, only this Holly saw it land on the side of Edwin's face.

Edwin didn't flinch. Holding his ground, he took Fury out in front. A neck in front. Half a length. There was no way Liam could catch him.

Edwin had won the Shergar Obstacle Race.

Minutes later, Holly joined him. Legs trembling, she dismounted and after giving Nessa a hug, she hurried over to Edwin and flung her arms around him.

'Brilliant, Edwin. You were brilliant.' Up close she saw an angry red mark on his cheek where Liam's whip had caught him. 'Are you all right? I saw what Liam did. Does it hurt?'

Everywhere was pandemonium. The Leper and Bonkers had their work cut out trying to calm the horses and examine them at the same time. Apart from Sean, who had sprained his ankle, none of the other children had been injured.

Holly had never seen the prince looking so grim and Mistoses was the picture of misery.

'This was all Vipereen's doing, I'm sure of it,' the prince said angrily.

Despite his triumphant win, Edwin was very quiet. 'I don't feel well, sis,' he said.

'I'm not surprised,' Holly said. 'That mark on your face must really hurt.'

'It's not that,' Edwin said. 'It's...I don't know...I feel...' and then he collapsed in a heap at Prince Rupert's feet.

A Mysterious Illness

Edwin was rushed back to the palace hospital by helicopter. Throughout the short journey, Edwin moaned and groaned and kept saying how sick he was. The minute they arrived the Leper proceeded to examine Edwin.

He scratched his head. 'This is a strange business and no mistake,' he muttered.

'What is it?' Holly demanded. 'Is he going to die? Is it to do with the race?'

'More likely something he's eaten or drunk very recently. Did you have anything different for breakfast?'

'No, just the usual seaweed stuff this morning.'

'Anything else after breakfast and before the race?'

'No, only that stuff you made Edwin drink. It must have been that that made him ill.'

The Leper made a dismissive gesture. 'Wouldn't have harmed him in the least. Just a little something to boost his energy level.'

Holly stared at the Leper. Was he telling the truth? Supposing the Leper was in league with Red Vipereen? What if it wasn't Mulch poisoning the food, but the Leper giving the horses something that made them sick? What if he was now getting to work on Edwin? And anyway, how could you trust anyone who was half a doctor and half a vet?

Edwin was tossing and turning and talking in a strange way. The Leper leaned over the bed trying to catch what he was saying.

'It's no good,' Holly said. 'He's talking a load of rubbish. Look, if you don't do something quick, I'm going to send for Prince Rupert.'

Her words galvanised the Leper into action. 'There's only one thing for it. Evil spirits must have entered Edwin's body. So, what we have to do is drive them out as quickly as possible. First off, we'll try a blanket wrap.'

'A blanket wrap. That doesn't sound much.'

The Leper coughed. 'Except I propose to try the wrap in conjunction with the Spirit Oven. A very special piece of equipment designed by Wizard Grindsniff. We've had some good results over the last couple of years using that combination.'

The blanket wrap looked exactly like the palace food: wide strips bound together formed a slithery sheet.

'It has special medicinal properties, you see,' the Leper said, 'which, when applied directly to the body, have a curative effect. But we must move quickly. There is no time to lose.

'I'm going to give Edwin a special injection that should calm him down. Then we'll apply the blanket wrap.'

Holly frowned. 'You're sure this injection won't make things worse.'

126

'He'll be fine, and he won't feel a thing. Probably have some pleasant dreams.'

Minutes later, after the injection, Edwin was fast asleep. Supervised by The Leper, two nurses wrapped Edwin's small body very tightly in the wrap leaving only his small white face visible. Edwin was then whisked along to the Spirit Oven that looked a bit like an enormous space capsule and wheeled inside. The Leper then got to work twiddling dials on an external panel.

'There, that should do the trick,' he announced.

Sitting on a bench beside The Leper, Holly listened to terrible moans and groans coming from the Oven. 'What's happening?' she demanded. 'It sounds like he's in pain.'

'Not at all,' the Leper said quietly. The evil spirits are being burned off.'

'Won't Edwin be burned as well?'

'Everything is proceeding well. Edwin will be quite unscathed.'

After forty minutes, Edwin was wheeled out and the wrap removed. The smell from it was disgusting.

'Now Edwin's body is breathing more easily, it is ready to absorb lots of good spirits,' The Leper explained.

With a long white gown wrapped around his body, Edwin was returned to the Spirit Oven. This time, Holly heard lots of sighs and whistling noises, like wind swishing through trees and peering through the glass portal, she saw Edwin floating in the air, a smile stretched from ear to ear.

Prince Rupert appeared demanding to know how things were going. He was reassured that everything was working out well and Edwin would soon be transferred to the recovery room.

Holly wasn't so confident. Ten minutes later, Edwin opened his eyes and looked around at the clinical white walls of the recovery room. 'Where am I? This is a hospital. What am I doing in hospital?'

'You were very ill, Edwin,' Holly said. 'Can you remember what happened?'

Edwin gave a weak smile. 'I remember winning the race.'

Prince Rupert beamed. 'You certainly did, Edwin, despite Red Vipereen's best efforts. Now we must do everything we can to get you fit and well, young man. In two days, we set out to search for Black. We must find him. It's our only hope.'

Wish Upon a Slab

Fully recovered, Edwin was able to complete the final two days of training.

On the eve of departure, Prince Rupert called a meeting. 'Edwin, you will ride Fury and Holly, you'll be pleased to hear that Grey is now fully recovered. Phelps has given her a clean bill of health, so I see no reason why you shouldn't take her.

'Mistoses, your horse will be Ercol, and I will take Ulysses. Pinch and Pouch will also accompany us. Any scents and those two will pick them up. We will also take Rory, old Grindsniff's trusty companion.'

At the mention of Rory, Holly pulled a face. She'd only seen the falcon once, but once had been enough.

'Something the matter?' Prince Rupert asked.

'Do we have to have Rory along?' Holly said. 'He doesn't seem to have helped Grindsniff much.'

'He brought back Grindsniff's map,' the prince reminded her. 'And, should the need arise, he could be very useful in relaying messages back to the palace. I suggest we also take along a palace guard.'

'How about Greton?' Mistoses suggested. 'She's very dependable.'

'Splendid idea.' The prince turned to Holly and Edwin. 'Greton is one of our finest and fittest guards. Hercules would be a suitable mount for her, I think. But now, you two, come along, it is time for the two of you to make your wishes.'

Prince Rupert led the way up several flights of stairs to the very top of the palace. They walked single file along a narrow corridor, passing through five doors that Prince Rupert unlocked and locked behind him each time until they came to a small chamber in the centre of which was a long, stone slab. The prince walked over to the side of the room and tapped on the wall. Instantly a part of the wall slid open to reveal a small cavity. Reaching inside, he drew out a ring and held it out for Holly and Edwin to inspect.

'Is that supposed to be special or something?' Holly said. ''Cos it doesn't look it.'

'This ring,' the prince said, his voice barely audible, 'has been in my family for centuries. This tiny object is going to help you realise your wishes. It once belonged to Greatorex, the greatest wizard of all time. Greatorex forged this ring with his own hands using gold and silver from deep inside a cave where he lived most of his life. Before he died, the wizard gave the ring to one of my forebears.' The prince pointed to the stone slab. That also belonged to Greatorex. On that he slept and, also sadly, died. I had the stone transported here.' He held out the ring to Edwin, 'Slip this on your middle finger and lie down on the stone. If you have strength and belief enough, your wish will come true.'

'But how will we know if it's worked?' Holly said.

Prince Rupert smiled. 'There will be a sign. An unmistakeable sign.'

Edwin took the ring and slid it onto his middle finger. 'It's a bit big. Does that matter?'

The words had no sooner left his mouth than he gave a shout. 'Hey, I can feel it getting smaller. I bet I won't be able to get it off now.'

'Don't worry,' the prince said. 'You will find that once you have made your wish, the ring will come off quite easily. Then it will be your turn, Holly.'

Edwin approached the stone slab warily.

'Don't be nervous,' the prince reassured. 'No harm will come to you. Now, remember, you must wish as hard as you can.'

Edwin had no sooner clambered up onto the slab and lain down, than Prince Rupert raised his arms over Edwin's prostrate body and, eyes closed, proceeded to chant: '*Dinayashatik, embrocathotek inveitiglio. Omvidio, margarlien, impositivitic zkelovadnik...*'

The silence in the small chamber was profound. Holly stared at her brother's body stretched out, looking for some sign that things were working. Seconds later, she thought she was seeing things. She blinked, then blinked again, unable to believe what she was seeing. Was Edwin's body really hovering in the air? She bent down and peered through the gap between Edwin's body and the stone slab. When she gasped, Prince Rupert shook his head and placed a finger to his lips.

The next time she blinked Edwin was lying flat on the slab again. He opened his eyes and looked at her. 'I must have gone to sleep and missed everything.'

'You probably did go to sleep,' the prince said. 'Your wish, whatever it was, will be granted, Edwin. But remember this. On no account must you tell anyone, not even your sister, what you wished for. If you tell someone, the wish may still come true, but at some point in the future there will be repercussions. Bad things may happen to you or the object of your wish. Of course, once your wish comes true, you are at liberty to say anything you want. Whether anyone will believe you is another matter.'

'Now, it's your turn, Holly.' The prince handed her the ring which, as he had predicted, had come off Edwin's finger easily. It was a bit too big for Holly as well, but no sooner had she slid it onto her finger than she felt it tighten until it fitted very snugly. She lay down on the slab, closed her eyes and, as the prince intoned the magic words, wished and wished with all her might. When she next opened her eyes, it was to find Edwin and the prince smiling at her.

'Well done,' Prince Rupert said. 'Successful in both cases. But do remember, both of you, on no account tell anyone your wishes.'

Keep-Safe Trinkets

At the crack of dawn Holly and Edwin were wide awake.

'We'll be off soon to find Black,' Edwin said. 'Can't wait.'

'Aren't you scared?'

'No, not really. It'll be great.'

'But just think for a minute. Wizard Grindsniff went off to the Wastelands and never came back.'

'That's because he went on his own. How stupid was that?'

'Yes, well, if Mum and Dad knew what was going on, they'd be mad. Aunt Bridget and Uncle Tom as well.

'Someone's got to find Black, and Madame Fosse said I was the one who could help.'

And that was as far as they got with the conversation because two guards appeared and whisked them off to Madame Fosse's psychitoreum.

Entering the psychitoreum was like being blinded by dazzling sunshine. Light bounced off walls that were encrusted with crystals.Holly and Edwin stood for a minute or two blinking as they adjusted to the brilliance.

'Come along,' Madame Fosse boomed. 'There's no time to waste.'She presented each of them with a rusty horseshoe, a gleaming, but dented pony brass and a ruby necklace.

'Carry these with you wherever you go,' she said. 'Wizard Grindsniff invested them with magical powers.'She sniffed. 'Such a pity the wizard didn't see fit to take them with him when he went haring off without so much as a by-your-leave. Considered himself too powerful to have need of such devices. Wizard Grindsniff was much too confident for his own good.'

'They don't look anything special,' Holly said.

'That's where you're wrong. The horseshoes will hit your target and immediately return to you. As for the pony brasses, hold them towards the sun and the enemy will be momentarily blinded.'

'What about the necklaces?' Holly said.

'You must keep them with you all the time. Wear them round your necks. They will help ward off evil.'

'Boys don't wear necklaces,' Edwin said.

'Some boys do,' Holly said. 'Look at all the pop stars. They aren't sissies. So just you get that necklace round your neck, Edwin Goodchild. We're going to need all the help we can get.'

But as Madame Fosse fixed the necklace round Edwin's neck, he clearly wasn't happy. And when the psychic clasped Edwin to her large bosom with much jingling and jangling, Holly expected him to explode with embarrassment.

'If nothing else, remember this,' Madame Fosse said. If you are bold enough, you can always call Vipereen's bluff.

'Now then, come along, Prince Rupert will be waiting.'

The psychic led the way to the stables where Prince Rupert and the rest of the search party were waiting for them. Holly was overjoyed to be reunited with Grey of Maccha who looked deep into Holly's eyes as if to say she knew exactly what was going on and what was expected of her. 'Glad you're better,' Holly whispered before planting a kiss on the horse's forehead.

There were seven of them, eight, if you counted Rory, perched on Prince Rupert's shoulder. Greton, blond hair flowing down to her waist and wearing a silver helmet and doublet, brought up the rear on Hercules as they made their way through the palace gardens. They were scarcely through the archway leading towards the training paddocks when loud cheering broke out. The whole palace had turned out to see them off, the only exceptions being Liam andSchlox. Liam couldn't stand the idea of Holly and Edwin holding centre stage, while Schlox was thought to be inconsolable at losing Black.

Prince Rupert, astride Ulysses, with Pouch tucked behind him, was looking very regal in flowing purple robes, while Mistoses on Ercol, with Pinch riding pillion, looked to the saddle born.

Patrick dashed over to wish Holly good luck and there were tears in Cate's eyes as she too waved goodbye.

'Take care,' she called after them.

The Search Begins

The palace grounds soon left far behind, the group trekked at a gentle pace through flat plains where the ground was hard and unyielding. The morning was bright and clear and Rory flying high, ahead of them, made an impressive sight against the blue of the sky. The other side of a shallow stream, the going became softer, the grass lush and greener. Prince Rupert pointed out hoof marks. No sooner had Pinch and Pouch begun sniffing around than they started jumping up and down in excitement. There was no doubt, they reported, Black had passed this way, and not all that long ago. Rory, soaring, circling, and dipping overhead, squawked approval and Mistoses, unable to execute a leap, settled for bobbing up and down in the saddle.

By midday, the sun had disappeared behind dark clouds, one very low black cloud hovering over what looked to be a forest. Drawing near, they saw that the forest was dense and overgrown as if no one had ever set foot inside. While Prince Rupert and Mistoses consulted Grindsniff's map, Holly and Edwin walked over to take a closer look at the trees that were laden with fruit.

'Cor, look at that. Carrots as well as apples growing on the trees,' Edwin yelled. 'And what are these brown things? Crikey, it's chocolate.'

'How weird,' Holly said.

'We could try a bit of chocolate?' About to reach up and grab a chocolate bar, a loud whinny from behind made him stop. Fury had followed them over to the trees. Another whinny from Fury and Edwin frowned. 'What's the matter?' he asked the horse. When the horse inclined his head, Edwin listened intently.

His eyes met Holly's. 'We mustn't eat this stuff,' he said. The words were no sooner out of his mouth than they saw Prince Rupert striding towards them.

'STOP,' the prince ordered. 'You haven't touched anything, have you?' he demanded.

'Edwin was going to try some chocolate,' Holly said, 'but he reckons Fury told him not to.'

'On no account.' Prince Rupert waved the map. 'Wizard Grindsniff named this forest Yummies Orchard, but he's written *Danger* next to it. He may have been referring to the stuff on the trees. I can't imagine how the wizard fathomed that out, but we must heed his warning. To help us all resist temptation, I suggest we eat and drink some of our own provisions.'

Hoping for something special, Edwin was disappointed when Greton started mixing some dried palace 'seaweed' with water. Despite being very hungry, he ate very slowly, his eyes fixed on the trees, imagining mouth-watering milk chocolate.

The map consulted again, Prince Rupert and Mistoses walked around the edge of the forest until they found a narrow track. While Rory was despatched to fly over the forest and meet them the other side, the rest of the party set off.

Picking their way along a narrow track that was overgrown in places, wasn't easy, the tight-packed trees blotting out light from the sky. Strange howling noises carried by the wind from the depths of the forest circled round them. As the wind grew stronger, it tore at their clothes and the howling grew louder. The branches of the trees, creaking like machines in need of oil, the search party was pelted with apples, carrots and chocolate. Tossing their heads, the horses reared and plunged in terror while Pinch and Pouch curled up in tight little balls and refused to move an inch.

As if things weren't bad enough, without any warning, Grey took it into her head to career off into uncharted territory. There was nothing Holly could do but cling on for dear life.

As Grey plunged deeper and deeper into the forest, trampling everything in her path. Holly crouched as low as she could to avoid being struck by overhanging branches. But how much longer could she hang on?

'Help! Help,' she cried as she slithered off Grey and landed in a bed of thistles and nettles. Dazed, and covered in scratches and blotches, she sat watching as Grey ploughed on until she came to a sudden halt.

Scrambling to her feet, Holly staggered over to the horse, standing stock still at the end of what looked like a bog. 'I know you haven't been well, Grey, and this is all a bit scary,' she scolded, 'but that was a stupid, horrid thing to do.'

Grey threw back her head and whinnied loudly in protest at being told off.

'The others will think I'm useless,' Holly went on. 'Prince Rupert might decide we have to go back to the palace. And you know what that means? Black may never be found, and The Mission may have to be cancelled. Just think, if Red Vipereen takes over the palace, you might find yourself without a stable and unemployed. My dad was out of work for ages and it's not much fun, I can tell you.'

Holly thought it was a bit stupid talking to a horse, but the funny thing was Grey quietened down and looked at Holly as if she'd understood every word.

As Holly was trying to get back on her horse, the others appeared.

'What happened to you?' Edwin shouted.

'What d'you think? I fell off. It happens to some of us, you know.'

'What are those big red blobs on the side of your face. Yuk, and your legs have got lots of red patches.'

'Stinging stuff, that's what and anyway, you've still got a big scar on your face.' (This wasn't strictly true since the scar had almost disappeared.)

'Are you all right,' Prince Rupert asked. 'I'll get Greton to dig out some lotion from the first-aid kit.'

'It's nothing,' Holly said. 'I'm all right, honestly. Let's get going, shall we? We've wasted enough time.'

'Hold on a minute.' Mistoses was busy examining the trunk of a tree. 'If I'm not mistaken these are horse hairs sticking to the tree. Black ones. Black of Saingland must have passed this way.'

The howling noises having died away, Pinch and Pouch were back in business. While Holly was having her scratches and blotches treated, the two gardeners scurried this way and that, button noses to the ground. A scent led them around the edge of the bog.

The other side of the bog, the forest fell away, and a vast wilderness opened up with mountains in the far distance. Rory, overhead, greeted their appearance with a couple of squawks.

Prince Rupert and Mistoses put their heads together over Grindsniff's map. The prince shook his head. 'I can't make this out at all. This spot, or very close to it, is clearly marked on the map by old Grindsniff as *Great Drop Off*. I don't know what it means, but we'd best be on our guard.'

Although the vegetation was lush and wild, they were able to gallop at full stretch until they came to the mountains. Prince Rupert led the way but was no more than halfway up when Rory, who'd flown on ahead, came back screeching his head off. No one could understand why he was making such a fuss, but they all became extra vigilant. Even so, they were unprepared for the shock that greeted them when they reached the top. The ground immediately in front of them dropped away so that they found themselves perched on the edge of a precipice.

Holly nearly died on the spot seeing how high up they were and how scary the drop was. Down below there was something that looked like a sheet of rusty, corrugated iron dotted with green mounds.

'This must be what Grindsniff meant by *Great Drop Off*,' Mistoses said.

'Be very careful, all of you,' Prince Rupert warned. 'Mind the horses don't take fright.'

Wheeling overhead, Rory suddenly plummeted down the mountain and landed on what looked like a sheet of corrugated rusty iron.

When Prince Rupert was sure everyone was safe and not in danger of losing their footing, he referred to the map again and pointed to where Rory was perched, bobbing up and down. 'Grindsniff called that Satsuma Sea. Those green mounds must be small islands. He's written GT on each of the islands, but what GT stands for I can't think.'

Pinch and Pouch sniffed the air for all they were worth, but neither of them could detect a scent.

'Somehow or other, we have to get down to the sea,' Prince Rupert said. 'I have no idea how Grindsniff managed it, but he certainly did because the trail he has marked out goes on for some considerable way.'

'Maybe he used magic,' Edwin said.

'More than likely,' the prince agreed.

Holly knew there was no way she was going down the side of the cliff, but she kept her thoughts to herself because Edwin was looking as perky as a parrot.

Prince Rupert was urging Ulysses towards the edge of the cliff, but sensible Ulysses wasn't having any of it. Digging his sturdy heels in, he refused to budge.

Then, before anyone could say 'Satsuma Sea', Edwin was setting his horse on the treacherous descent. Head held high, he shouted words of encouragement not only to Fury but to the others. 'Don't be frightened. It's not as hard as it looks. Follow me.'

Prince Rupert with Pouch, who had his eyes closed, followed tentatively. Mistoses came up alongside Holly and nodded for her to join the procession.

'Come on, come on,' Holly muttered to herself. 'If Edwin can do it, so can you.'

She risked glancing down the cliff-side and that was her big mistake. Also, the light was fading. There was no way she was going to make it. So what if Edwin was traipsing down the cliff like Spiderman on horseback, she had absolutely no intention of following his lead.

Halfway down, Edwin paused and looked back. He cupped his hands over his mouth and yelled. 'Come on Holly. Don't be a wimp.'

That did it. No way was she going to be called a wimp by Edwin. Without giving herself time to think, she spurred Grey of Maccha forward who, judging by her quivering body and flaring nostrils, was every bit as nervous as she was.

Time stood still as Holly eased her way down. At one point, Grey lost her footing, and they slithered a terrifyingly long way.

It took an age for Holly to reach the bottom. When she did, Mistoses did one of his famous leaps. Holly might have joined him, except everyone was looking very serious and watching intently as Pinch and Pouch dashed in and out of the waves by the edge of the water. After half an hour or so, the gardeners admitted defeat. The trail had gone cold. It looked as if the death-defying descent down the side of the cliff had all been for nothing.

Prince Rupert, however, refused to be dismayed. 'I suggest we set up camp for the night. Brains are at their sharpest in the morning.'

Untangling the horses' tails and picking out bits of twigs and burrs from their coats took a long time, but finally, nearly dying of starvation, everyone, horses and Rory included, was tucking into reconstituted 'seaweed'.

With night closing in, it was getting cold. Greton gathered driftwood from along the shore and lit a fire and, for a while, they sat bunched together warming their toes. Pinch produced a very small flute and began playing strange tunes which made everyone feel relaxed. Mistoses, in a very high-pitched voice, began singing the Ballad of Wizard Grindsniff.:

Old Grindsniff was a wizard,
the best in all the land,
but he grew too big for his own big boots
and was slain by an unknown hand

He was raised by the sands of Donegal
where the waves went rolling by.

He spoke with the fairies at Dingly Dell
and studied the stars in the sky

He could conjure a fire from nothing at all,
change goats or sheep into hens.
With a magic wand he could freeze a lake
and all this he'd learned by age ten.

Over four hundred years he lived on earth
and ne'er was a wizard so good.
He would cure the sick and heal the lame,
always doing the best that he could.

Yes, old Grindsniff was a wizard,
the best in all the land,
but he grew too big for his own big boots
and was slain by an unknown hand.

As Mistoses' voice died away, Prince Rupert wiped a tear from his eyes and said in a gruff voice that they had all better get some sleep. Holly was just wondering where they were supposed to sleep when Prince Rupert handed each of them a bright silk square which, at the pull of a cord, billowed out to form a bell tent.

The very last thing the prince did was to send Rory off into the night sky and over Satsuma Sea in the hope the falcon might pick up the trail.

Up Against a Brick Wall

Rays from the morning sun cast a strange, phosphorescent glow over the sea. But it wasn't this that had everyone gawking by the water's edge. Mr Mistoses was standing on one of the green islands out at sea yelling and dancing like a lunatic. It took a while to make out what he was shouting.

'The islands aren't islands. The islands aren't islands.' he was shouting.

The group on the shore focused on the green mound where Mistoses was standing. Had the palace secretary taken leave of his senses?

Prince Rupert cupped his hands and shouted back, 'What are you up to? We haven't time for you frolicking about.'

'It's not an island,' Mistoses hollered back.

Prince Rupert raised his eyes to heaven as if to say, 'the strain has been too much for the palace secretary'.

As they continued to stare, an amazing thing happened. The island Mistoses was leaping about on started moving. An optical illusion, or what? Because, slowly, very very slowly, the island came towards them.

As it glided right up to the shore, Mistoses jumped off and leapt into the air:

Grandmother Moses and Mr Mistoses
Sunlight and roses, anything goses
For Mr Mistoses.

Arms akimbo, Prince Rupert stood appraising the island that appeared to have come to greet them. 'A turtle,' he declared. 'Would you believe it, it's a giant green turtle in an orange sea. Grindsniff's GT must stand for 'Giant Turtle'.

'But does it help us as to where we should be going next?' Holly said. There were times she was sure she was the only person in the world with any sense.

'We could have a turtle ride,' Edwin exclaimed.

'Wowee,' Pinch and Pouch yelled in unison.

'I didn't think we'd come all this way to play games,' Holly said starchily. She didn't fancy the idea of sailing across an orange sea on a giant green turtle. Supposing it turned turtle? Where would that leave them? Drowned at the bottom of the horrid Satsuma Sea, no doubt.

Prince Rupert was pondering what to do next when Mistoses began dancing again and pointing to the sky. Looking up, the travellers saw a huge flock of white doves flying overhead and heading seaward. As they continued to gaze upwards, the birds broke rank only to immediately regroup in a tighter formation.

'Look, an arrow,' Edwin cried. 'They've formed the shape of an arrow.'

'You're right.' Mistoses gave a bouncy leap and consulted a pocket compass. 'And it's pointing across the sea in a north-easterly direction.'

'And how are we to go in that direction?' Holly said.

Mistoses and Edwin started giggling.

'By turtle, I should think,' Prince Rupert said, treating Holly to a gleaming smile.

In the twinkling of an eye, they were all packed up and, ready to set sail; all piled on top of a turtle's back which was big enough to take a houseful of furniture, if not the house itself. And, as if it knew exactly what was going on, the turtle set sail, following the arrow in the sky.

Holly was struck by a thoroughly gloomy and miserable thought. Supposing it was all a hoax and they were sailing into a trap. Supposing the doves and the turtles, and this turtle, in particular, were in league with Red Vipereen.

They sailed a great distance but going so slowly, it took the best part of the day. It was late afternoon before land was sighted at the tip of the feathery arrow. As soon as they had disembarked, the flock of doves wheeled around and flew off into the distance. Rory flew down and landed on Prince Rupert's shoulder where he sat throwing nasty looks at Holly and Edwin.

There was something about the falcon that made Holly's flesh crawl even though he had come to the rescue.

These thoughts went clean out of her mind when Pinch and Pouch picked up the scent of Black again. After having some food, they set off once more. With Pinch and Pouch leading the way, they followed the trail for a mile or so until they came to a vast wall with a stout round door in the middle. But although they banged as loud as they could, there was no answer. The door stayed stubbornly shut. There was no way they could climb over the wall because it soared way up into the sky with no hint of a foothold. Thinking they could find a way around it, they followed the wall in one direction only to discover it was never ending and, trying the other way, found the same thing. By this time, it was growing dark and everyone, especially Edwin who was yawning his head off, was needing sleep.

Prince Rupert consulted Grindsniff's map, which having been referred to so often, was getting tatty round the edges. Sure enough, the map showed a very high wall stretching from one side of the map to the other and underneath Grindsniff had written: *The Never-ending Wall.* The wizard had also scrawled a few lines, but it was getting dark and with so many creases in the paper, the words were hard to read. It was decided to leave it until the morning.

Caught in a Web

As dawn was breaking, Prince Rupert spread the map out on the ground, and everyone crowded round. After an hour or so of holding the map first this way and then that, they finally deciphered the message:

Under or over
You'll not land in clover
Try here or try there
And you'll tear out your hair
So, open the shute
With three toots on a flute

The prince frowned, trying to make sense of the riddle. 'So, what was our old wizard getting at?'

'Seems clear as anything to me,' Holly said. 'It means you have to blow on a flute three times to get the door to open.'

'But where...?' They all turned to look at Pinch, who produced his small flute with a flourish.

Everyone gathered round the stout door in the wall as Pinch gave three toots. Immediately, the door vanished and all of them, travellers, horses, equipment and food provisions, and even Rory, who hated having his feathers ruffled, were sucked into a huge wind tunnel. But what they had expected would be a terrifying experience turned out to be rather enjoyable. It was like floating in space. It was so enjoyable Holly didn't want it to end but end it did when they all landed in an untidy heap in the middle of a cavernous chamber with three passageways leading off it. Grindsniff's map gave no indication of which passage they should take. In fact, it gave no clue at all as to what kind of building they were in.

'We'll each have to take a passageway,' Prince Rupert said. 'See if any of them lead us out the other side.'

It was decided that Pinch and Mistoses, should take one passage, Pouch and Prince Rupert the second one and Holly, Edwin and Greton, the third.

Holly peered down one of the dark, cavernous passages. 'You can't see a thing.'

Rummaging amongst the equipment scattered all over the floor, Prince Rupert came up with three torches. 'Here we are. One for each group. Now, any sign of danger you get yourselves back here double quick. If, for any reason, you can't get back, shout as loud as you can and the rest of us will come running.'

The children and Greton set off but had not got very far when they realised that both Fury and Grey weren't happy. The torch wasn't giving much light and the horses' steps were getting shorter and shorter. Finally, all three horses braced their legs and refused to take another step. No matter how hard they were urged on, the horses wouldn't budge.

'We have to go back,' Edwin said. 'Fury and Grey are saying something's wrong.'

'We might as well see how far we can get,' Holly said.' If anything happens, all we have to do is shout and the others will be here.'

'Well, I'm not going any further,' Edwin said firmly. 'You can if you like.'

'You stay here with the horses then,' Greton suggested.

Holly and Greton moved cautiously forward, on foot, Holly shining the torch on the ground. No more than a few yards further on, they stopped dead at the edge of a yawning chasm. Very carefully, Holly squatted down as close to the edge as she dared but there was not enough light to show how deep the hole was. Miles deep for all she knew.

When they rejoined Edwin, Holly gave each of the horses a hug. 'Thank you,' she said. 'It's a good job you warned us.'

'Listen,' Edwin said. 'What's that noise?'

Very faintly they heard a cry. 'Help, help.' At first Holly thought it was coming from the bottom of the pit, before realising it was from somewhere behind them. As they were remounting the horses, Prince Rupert, with Pouch, came riding up to them. 'Thank goodness you're safe,' he gasped. 'Thought we heard you calling.'

'Help, help,' the yells came again. They could also hear horses whinnying in distress.

'Mistoses,' they all said together.

Two hundred yards down the passage Mistoses and Pinch had taken, they came to large chamber, daylight streaming down through an enormous fissure in the ceiling, and found their companions, together with Ercol, all tangled up in a giant spider's web. Ercol was screaming with fright and Mistoses was wailing: 'Oh helpless and hapless Mistoses'. Pinch, completely silent and motionless was curled up in a tiny ball.

'Don't worry, we'll soon have you out,' Prince Rupert said, getting straight to work on the strands with a sharp dagger. Greton used her teeth to cut through the strong webbing while Holly and Pouch joined in using their bare hands. At the rate they were going, it would take forever.

Edwin did what he could to calm Ercol who was snorting loudly. 'Don't be scared. We'll soon have you free. Keep still. There now, there now.' Ercol gave a long tremor before quietening down.

'Look out, look out,' Mistoses shouted.

Looking up, they saw hundreds of giant spiders crawling through the crevice and creeping down the sides of the chamber towards them. Once again, the horses began panicking. And again, Edwin spoke to them until they calmed down. But all the while the spiders were getting closer and closer. Holly was thinking they couldn't possibly escape when a deafening noise broke out. She pressed her hands to her ears. How could spiders make such a din?

'It's not the spiders,' Edwin said. 'Look it's Rory.' Sure enough, Rory, leading a flock of pigeons, was zooming through the crevice towards them. Holly couldn't believe how relieved she felt at the sight of the falcon.

Rory and the pigeons lost no time getting to work. Under a savage onslaught, the spiders gasped and shrivelled to next to nothing before disappearing altogether. The birds then made short shrift of breaking through the gigantic web to free the prisoners.

While Edwin continued to soothe the horses, Prince Rupert produced the hip flask given to him by Madame Fosse and took a long draught. Mistoses and Pinch also took several gulps and immediately sprang back to life, Pinch joining Pouch in sniffing around.

'Got a whiff of anything?' Mistoses asked.

Sniff, sniff, sniff.

'They're onto something or my name's not Mr. Mistoses.'

Pinch punched the air. 'The trail,' he cried in his tiny reedy voice. 'We have the trail again.'

Edwin the Brave

A mile or so along the trail, they emerged into the open – the strangest and starkest landscape imaginable - at least from the glimpses they caught through a mist that swirled and twirled all around them. According to Grindsniff's map, this was *Moon Base* with *Dragon Bridge* close by.

Pinch and Pouch scampered on ahead and came back minutes later, their eyes wide with fear and the news that they were walking along a mountain ledge. A few steps to the right and they would plunge into a ravine. The two gardeners had also discovered up ahead, a narrow bridge spanning a gaping canyon.

Walking in single file, leading the horses, the party edged their way along the ledge towards the bridge that close to, proved to be no ordinary bridge, but something constructed from dark, slimy green scales. The mist lifting for a few seconds, they caught a glimpse of the bed of the canyon and the sight of an army of dragons down below blowing wreaths of smoke. The mist wasn't a mist at all. It was dragon smoke.

'D'you think the bridge is made out of dragon scales?' Edwin asked.

'Looks like it,' Prince Rupert said. 'Most likely the work of a certain someone we know.'

Everyone knew he meant Red Vipereen, but in the silence and the fog, no one dared say his name aloud.

'And if he slayed dragons so as to construct the bridge, you can bet the remaining dragons will have it in for anyone trying to cross that bridge.'

Pinch and Pouch had no doubts that Black of Saingland had been over the bridge, but being too fearful to cross it themselves, it was left for Prince Rupert and Ulysses to make the first attempt. But Ulysses, one of the bravest horses in the palace stables, was having none of it. Undaunted, Prince Rupert set out to cross on his own, but the minute he set foot on *Dragon Bridge* it began swaying so violently he was in danger of being flung over the side.

'It's no good,' he said grimly. 'There's no way we can cross. Far too dangerous. It's not as if we can even get down the mountain and up the other side. The dragons would have something to say about that.'

Mistoses looked glum. 'How the devil did Grindsniff manage it, I wonder?'

'Wizardry. That's how,' Prince Rupert said.

'If Black of Saingland went that way,' Edwin cut in. 'We should be able to get across as well.'

'Yes, but Black was probably in the company of you know who,' Prince Rupert said. 'A thoroughly evil, but dastardly clever wizard.'

'We can't just let Vipereen win,' Edwin said.

'We don't have any choice,' Holly said.

There was a long, long silence during which everyone racked their brains for an idea.

Edwin was the first to break the silence.

'I think I could get over with Fury,' he said quietly.

Holly turned chalk white. 'And just what do you think you'd do the other side on your own? That's if you did make it to the other side, which is extremely doubtful. If Vipereen or any of the witches are over there, they'll make mincemeat of you.'

'Come with me, then,' Edwin urged.

Holly's blood froze. 'That's the stupidest idea you've had in your entire life, Edwin Goodchild. I wouldn't cross that bridge for all the money in the world.'

'Quite right.' Prince Rupert backed her up instantly. 'I said at the outset that should our lives be in jeopardy we would turn back. And that, I'm afraid is what we must do. Black is a very special horse, but I can't risk lives trying to get him back. All we can do is hope he is being well cared for.'

Edwin was playing with the ruby necklace round his neck. 'Madame Fosse said these necklaces would keep us safe.'

Prince Rupert gave a pained laugh. 'I'm afraid you'd need more than a keep-safe necklace to get you over that bridge.'

'I just know I can do it,' Edwin said quietly. 'But I want Holly with me, 'cos she's right. I wouldn't know what to do the other side on my own.'

Holly tried to make herself as small as Pinch and Pouch who were huddled together in a tight ball.

Mistoses was wringing his hands, too upset to speak.

'There's no way you're going across that bridge,' Prince Rupert said firmly.

But before anyone realised what was happening, Edwin was leading Fury towards *Dragon Bridge*. 'Come on, Holly,' Edwin called, commandingly. 'Follow me.' He reached out an arm and, Holly didn't know how or why it happened, but the next thing she was up and astride Fury, behind Edwin. They were on the bridge, and it was rocking dangerously from side to side. Any minute, Holly thought, and they'd go hurtling over the side to be burned alive or eaten by the dragons. And even if they didn't get flung over the side, the bridge might snap in two, or dragon breath might set it on fire. Behind, Prince Rupert was roaring for them to turn back, and Grey of Maccha was whinnying in despair.

'Whatever you do, don't look down,' Edwin shouted over his shoulder.

Holly forced herself to look straight ahead, peering through the smoke for a glimpse of firm ground the other side.

'There's a good boy,' Edwin stroked Fury. 'Come on, Fury. Atta boy, we can do it. Not far now.'

It wasn't until the swaying finally stopped and Fury gave a high triumphant neigh that Holly realised they had reached the other side. They were safe!

For the first time, Holly and Edwin looked back but it was hard to make out the rest of the search party because of all the billowing dragon smoke.

'So now what do we do?' Holly said. 'We haven't got Pinch and Pouch to pick up the scent. We should have brought Grindsniff's map. It was the daftest thing ever dashing off like that.'

Edwin patted his pockets. 'We've still got the horseshoes and things,' he said. 'We'll just have to go on and hope for the best.'

'Yes, but which way. We haven't got Pinch and Pouch to help us. We could go on for miles and just get ourselves lost.'

Edwin pointed to a steep path, sloping downwards. 'That's the only path I can see.'

How come Edwin who was one year and one month younger and had always been the biggest wimp out, was taking control? No one back at school would ever believe it. Not even Mum and Dad or Uncle Tom and Aunt Bridget would believe it.

'D'you know what, Edwin Goodchild, you're just like Wizard Grindsniff. You've become too big for your boots. Anyway, just don't blame me if we find ourselves in a mess.'

A Dark Surprise

The path led through a small wood and over a range of gentle, undulating hills. It was starting to get dark when they came to a shallow stream. They stopped for a while to let Fury take a drink and had a few sips themselves. Crystal clear, the water tasted like honey. They took deep gulps, splashed water on their faces and immediately felt much better.

'We should have brought some food,' Edwin said. 'I'm really hungry.'

The words were scarcely out of his mouth when a small package, dropped from the sky, knocked him sideways. Overhead Rory gave a loud squawk before flying off into the distance.

The package contained lots of palace dried 'seaweed' and a plastic bottle of palace water to mix with it to make it edible. After feeding Fury, they were so hungry that they just gobbled the food down without even bothering to imagine their favourite food.

No more than a hundred yards ahead was another hill where Holly suggested they should rest for the night. By now it was so dark that it was only when they were up close to the hill that they made out a black tent pitched about halfway up where the hill plateaued out. The tent would not have been visible but for a small lantern hanging by the entrance. It was the first sign of human life they'd come across since setting out over the Grindsniff Wastelands.

'Brilliant,' Edwin said, already making his way up the hill. 'We might be able to camp there for the night. Come on, sis. They might have some proper food as well.'

Holly stared through the gloom at the dark shape on the hill. 'But who on earth would be camping out here?'

'Could be scouts or something.'

'You do say some stupid things, Edwin,' Holly snapped. 'No one is supposed to know this place exists. I don't like the look of it.'

Leading Fury, they trudged wearily up the hill. The nearer they got to the tent, the bigger it looked, and Holly's heart gave a sudden lurch because close to the tent resembled a black witch's hat.

'If it's empty, maybe we could stay inside anyway,' Edwin said.

The entrance to the tent was gaping wide. Edwin stuck his head inside. 'Wow, it's really big,' he called to Holly over his shoulder. 'You could get loads of people inside.' And then he shot back out like a bullet. 'Guess what?' he said in a trembly voice. 'There are all these big, black cauldrons. Just like there was at...'

'...the Holding Bay.' Holly gulped.

A flicker of light in the sky made Holly look up. A ghostly silver moon was gliding into view. The moon provided no more than a sliver of light, but it was enough to pick out a long row of biker witches strung out on the crest of the hill.

Holly shrieked, but Edwin was already mounting Fury. His small voice rang out in the night. 'Come on, Holly, get up behind me,' he ordered 'Quick as you can.'

Somehow, Holly did as she was told, but then to her amazement, instead of Edwin taking flight downhill, he urged Fury upwards, straight towards the enemy. Within a few feet of the witches, Edwin yelled, 'do it, Fury, do it.' And leaving the ground behind, they soared through the air, higher and higher, right over a row of sharp, noses pointed skyward.

'How about that?' Edwin giggled.

'Stop it, Edwin,' Holly shouted. 'Stop giggling or you'll have us both off.'

No sooner had they hit the ground than Edwin had Fury racing down the other side of the hill as fast as his sturdy legs would go. A noise like thunder broke out. The witches were revving up and would soon be on top of them. They didn't stand a chance. The bikes were gaining on them fast. Nearer and nearer. Louder and louder. In no time, they were surrounded, the biker witches swooping and diving all around. Stretched to his limits, Fury reared and plunged. Arms around her brother's waist, Holly clung on grimly.

The noise of cackling witches was terrifying. A sharp nose prodded Holly's arm, then her thigh.

'I'm going to try something,' Edwin shouted. He dug into his pocket, brought out his horseshoe and flung it at the nearest witch. Caught squarely on the chin, the witch toppled off her bike and the horseshoe promptly returned to Edwin's outstretched hand.

'It works,' Edwin shouted.

Trying to cling onto Edwin with one hand, Holly groped around for her own horseshoe and flung it.

Time and again the two of them flung the horseshoes, sometimes hitting and sometimes toppling a witch, but they weren't going to be able to hold out for long. There were too many witches and not enough horseshoes.

A high-pitched screech made Holly look up. Rory was flying directly above them, but what was he trying to say?

In the nick of time, Edwin gathered Fury for another flying leap across a looming whirlpool. Once more, they were airborne, but so were the witches, right alongside them.

Diving and screeching and pecking, Rory was doing everything he could to scare the witches. He was making a very odd sound indeed. *Coo...coo...*

As if they weren't in enough trouble, Holly saw a white mist rolling steadily towards them. They were thundering into a blinding snowstorm. But when the storm arched to form a long tunnel, Holly realised it wasn't a snowstorm at all, but a flock of white doves come to the rescue.

Safely through the tunnel of doves, they both stopped to look back. The cries of the birds mingled with the screech of witches reached a deafening crescendo, a great battle raging between black and white.

The battle went on for a very long time, so long that it was starting to get light, rays of the morning sun breaking on the horizon.

'Hey, you know what? We didn't even sleep last night,' Edwin remarked, 'but it's funny 'cos I don't feel a bit tired. Fury feels the same. Look at him.'

The dark horse was stamping his feet, and champing at the bit, eager to be on the move.

'What's wrong, Fury,' Edwin asked. 'What is it?'

'He wants to get clean away from the witches, that's what,' Holly said.

Edwin shook his head. 'No. There's something up ahead that's getting him all stirred up.'

Giving Fury a free rein, they went on. Fury led them through a wood and across flat meadowland, stopping twice to give a couple of whinnies. The second time, Holly and Edwin heard, or thought they heard, a single long whinny in response. In the distance, they made out a barn and in front of the barn was a black horse, forelegs waving the air.

'Crikey,' Edwin said.

Holly held her breath.

They rode as fast as they could over to the barn. Yes, there was no mistake. Black of Saingland, tethered to a post, lifted his majestic head, and gave a hearty greeting, loud enough to wake the dead, but not, seemingly, the two witches guarding him, who lay spread-eagled on a pile of hay, heads resting on their motorbikes.

After telling Fury to remain quiet, Edwin quickly dismounted and made his way over to Black. 'Don't worry, Black; he whispered. 'We'll soon have you free and back home.

Holly came up alongside him. 'Now what do we do?' She sized up the situation. A padlock was keeping Black chained to the post, the key to which had to be in that big bunch of keys Holly could see hanging from a belt round one of the witches. But how to get hold of the key without waking them?

'You stay here, Edwin,' Holly said. 'Keep an eye open for the rest of the witches. I'll try and get the key.'

She crept towards the witches. As if knowing what was going on, Black stood motionless, a fierce gleam in his dark eyes.

Nearer and nearer. Holly was so close to the witch with the key she could smell her foul breath. When the witch gave a sudden and violent twitch, Holly waited until she had settled again before kneeling down and reaching towards the keys.

A shout from Edwin was accompanied by a huge zig-zaggy blaze of light in the sky. Holly knew there was no time to lose. She dived for the keys, but they were tightly attached to the belt and, as Holly wrestled to get them free, the witch woke and gave a piercing shriek. Holly continued tugging at the keys, but with the witch clawing and jabbing at her with her sharp nose, she lost her grip. The other witch, now wide awake, joined in the action. But so did Edwin. Holding his pony brass on high, it caught the rays of the morning sun and instantly, one of the witches recoiled, clutching at her eyes.

When Holly did the same with her own pony brass, both the witches were momentarily blinded, and Holly was able to wrest the keys free. Joining in the fray, Fury kicked out at the witches and managed to bite one of them. As the witches rolled on the ground in agony, Holly got to work trying one key after another in the padlock.

A second great flash of lightning zig-zagged down towards Holly, so powerful this time, that she blacked out.

It was several minutes before she came round. When she did, she saw Edwin waving a key in the air and Black, free as the wind, was racing round the paddock. But the victory was short-lived. Another flash of light and Red Vipereen in his full wizard regalia complete with tall, pointed hat, stood right in front of Holly. Red eyes boring into her, Holly shrivelled and watched, petrified, as Vipereen raised his arms and swirled around creating more flashes of light out of which emerged four hideous shapes. Four, blue-tinged skeleton horses, so terrifying they had Holly glued to the spot. Skeleton hooves would have trampled her to death if it hadn't been for Edwin, astride Black, yelling at her to mount Fury.

Dazed, Holly managed to do as instructed and, instantly, Black and Fury were off at a lick, tearing off across the meadowland. With the skeleton horses in rattling pursuit, Holly gritted her teeth and clung on for dear life.

'Black knows the way. I'm giving him his head,' Edwin shouted to her as they raced across open country.

But some of the skeleton horses, with no weight to carry, started gaining on them, the sound of thundering hooves and clanking bones getting closer and closer. Edwin hurled his horseshoe at one of the skeletons. The horseshoe passed straight through the bones and returned to Edwin's hand. From overhead came the roar of motorbikes. Rory and the doves had held off the witches for as long as they possibly could, but the witches had broken free and were on their motorbikes in pursuit again.

Holly tugged at the necklace round her neck and as one of the witches came hurtling towards her, she whirled the necklace round and round. Immediately the witch retreated.

When Edwin did the same, the witch closest to him fell back.

Making horrible, gurgling noises the skeleton horses were closing fast and the witches, hundreds of them now, were diving down from the sky. Ahead, another obstacle loomed in the shape of a towering and unscalable rock face, with no magic door this time that would open at the toot of a flute. It was hopeless. This is it, Holly decided.

'Hey look.' Edwin pointed towards the cliff.

As if by magic, an opening had appeared and standing by the opening was a very old man with bright blue eyes in a round, lined face, and white fuzzy hair. He was wearing a blue flowing robe and a blue and white pointed hat. A wide smile on his wizened face, he was beckoning them.

Through the opening they zoomed and were no sooner inside than the entrance closed behind them, and the old man, whoever he was, had not followed them in.

It was not only light inside the cave but quite warm and feeling like they were wrapped in a huge comfort blanket, Holly and Edwin settled down for the night.

The last thing Edwin said before going to sleep was, 'Who d'you think that old man was?'

'Don't know,' Holly said sleepily. She did have an idea but decided it would have to wait until they got back to Prince Rupert and the others. That's if they ever did make it back.

The Return Journey

Refreshed after a long sleep, Holly and Edwin left it to Black to lead them along a narrow craggy path that wound and twisted its way through the cave for over a mile and a half. Finally, they came to the end of the path, only to find an impenetrable wall of rock in front of them.

'Now what do we do?' Edwin asked.

The words were no sooner out of his mouth than the rock wall vanished and there in front of them were green fields bathed in strong sunlight and stretching far into the distance.

Not a whiff of a witch or a skeleton horse, although that didn't necessarily mean they were out of danger, not by any means. Black continued to lead the way as if he knew exactly where he was going. Unhindered, the return journey was much quicker than the outward one, but even so, it took the best part of a day and by the time they reached *Dragon Bridge*, dusk had fallen.

The smoke around *Dragon Bridge* had thinned out giving a clear view of hundreds of slumbering dragons on the bed of the canyon. Holly dreaded to think what might happen if the dragons woke up and began breathing fire again. The quicker they got across the bridge the better.

Before they reached the other side of the bridge, Mistoses was flinging himself into the air so violently he was in danger of harming himself. Pinch and Pouch were waving and hugging each other and Greton was punching the air for all she was worth. All this was done in absolute silence, no one wanting to disturb the dragons. Prince Rupert was standing motionless, worried sick, Holly guessed, about the two of them managing to safely recross the treacherous bridge.

Now whether it was because the dragons were asleep or some strange power was protecting Holly and Edwin, it's hard to say, but the bridge didn't budge an inch as they made their way across.

When they reached the other side, Mistoses leapt into the air and burst into song:

Wigglemanoses and ticklematoeses
It's moonlight and roses
For Mr Mistoses

Holly could see Prince Rupert was trying to maintain a stern expression, but his large brown eyes were brimming with gratitude.

'This is such a proud moment,' Greton said, giving Holly and Edwin a hug. Black too came in for lots of hugs. Neither was Fury overlooked in the hugs department.

'Thank God you're safe,' Prince Rupert said. 'But that was very irresponsible of the two of you going off like that. However, I cannot thank you enough for rescuing Black. Now you must rest, eat and if you're up to it, tell us what happened.' He led the way to a large, dry cave, spacious enough to accommodate horses and all.

No sooner had they eaten, than Edwin fell fast asleep, but Holly forced herself to stay awake. In her element, being the centre of attention, she had everyone hanging on her every word as she told of their adventures.

'But with the witches chasing us, we really thought we'd had it when we came smack bang up against this rock wall. We could never have climbed up it,' Holly said.

'So, what happened?' the prince asked.

'First, there was just this great big rock in front of us and next, there was an opening. and there was this old man with a blue robe and pointed hat. It was as if he'd created the opening for us.'

Prince Rupert leaned forward his eyes alight. 'What did he look like?'

'Very old with sort of frizzy white hair and a round face with lots of wrinkles and he wasn't very tall.'

Tears welled in the prince's eyes. 'Grindsniff, he said softly. 'Wizard Grindsniff.'

'I thought it might be,' Holly said.

'But where is he? Why isn't he with you?'

Holly shook her head. 'One minute he was there and the next thing he'd gone.'

'Did he have a halo of flashing stars around his head? Think carefully.'

Holly shook her head. 'No, there was nothing like that.'

'Ah, then there's no question. Grindsniff must have passed on. No doubt it was his ghost you saw. Somehow our old wizard found a means of helping you.' A tear trickled down Prince Rupert's face and Mistoses was dabbing at his eyes with a corner of his bell tent.

'The other odd thing is that Black seemed to have the route back all worked out.'

'Grindsniff would have been directing him,' Mistoses said. 'Helped you cross that bridge safely, as well.'

Prince Rupert said 'After you left, we tried several times to cross it, but there was no way any of us could make it. Good old Grindsniff. We owe him so much.'

After a good night's rest, everyone was ready for the return trip which, Prince Rupert explained would be via a different route. 'Mistoses and I have been studying Grindsniff's map and it looks as if we ought to be able to circumnavigate *Great Drop Off* and *Yummies Orchard* by taking a different route via turtle across the *Satsuma Sea.* We will, however, still have *The Never-ending Wall* to contend with.'

'So long as we don't run into any more spiders,' Mistoses said, 'I hate spiders.'

'It's the witches I'm bothered about, 'Holly said. 'They can't be that far behind.'

Edwin rode Black for part of the way before switching to Fury, but Holly stuck with Grey. At the door of *The Neverending Wall*, Pinch gave three toots on his flute and this time *The Neverending Wall* completely disappeared. As if the wall and the chambers and passageways inside had never existed.

So far so good. Everything was going so smoothly, too smoothly for Holly's liking. She was forever looking over her shoulder expecting to spot witches or skeleton horses closing in.

When they reached the Satsuma Sea, Mistoses clapped his hands and a Giant Turtle glided slowly over. They all piled on top of the turtle's back and had no sooner unsaddled the horses than they were off across the rolling orange sea. The turtle moved slowly at first, but swimming with the tide, soon picked up speed and leaving all the other Giant Turtles behind, hit the open sea. The wind was quite sharp and ominous dark clouds scurried overhead. In the nick of time, before it bucketed down, they had the waterproof bell tents in place, including ones big enough for the horses.

Holly hadn't realised how much the expedition had exhausted her, and despite her anxiety about the witches and Red Vipereen, she felt so snug inside her tent that she fell fast asleep. How long she slept she didn't know but the next thing she knew, Edwin was shaking her awake.

'We've landed,' he said. 'Prince Rupert says that if we set off now, we've a good chance of getting to the palace before its dark.'

Rubbing sleep from her eyes, Holly emerged from her tent and started helping pack everything away. Prince Rupert was busy scribbling a message for Rory to take to the palace. 'There,' he said, watching the bird take to the skies. 'I've let them know we're safe and sound, and on our way back. That should set everyone's minds at rest.'

'Have you told them about Black?' Edwin asked.

'I have indeed,' the prince said.

As they completed the last leg of their journey, the prince suggested they should sing the palace horse anthem to keep up their spirits. Holly and Edwin had never heard the anthem before, but they soon picked up the chorus and joined in the second time around.

Fleet of foot and stout of heart
Till journey's end they play their part
Loyal and steadfast, ever true
Always putting their trust in you

Whoa, whoa, whoa...

(Chorus)
When the times are rough
And the going gets tough
They will still be there.
When the days are long
And things go wrong
They will comfort you.
If our lives are rushed
And our dreams are crushed
They will lift you up...
And when you're old and grey
And you're fading away
They will still love you.

Whoa, whoa, whoa...

Majestic soul and noble mind
A better friend is hard to find
And never creature was so bold
Since days of yore, we have been told

Whoa, whoa, whoa...

When the times are rough
And the going gets tough
They will still be there...
When the days are long
And things go wrong
They will comfort you
If our lives are rushed
And our dreams are crushed
They will lift you up...
And when you're old and grey
And you're fading away
They will still love you...

Whoa, whoa, whoa...

Sound of wind and strong of limb
A shining light that will not dim
So sing the hills and valleys low
So sing us all and onward go

Whoa, whoa, whoa...

When the times are rough
And the going gets tough
They will still be there...
When the days are long
And things go wrong
They will comfort you
If our lives are rushed
And our dreams are crushed
They will lift you up
And when you're old and grey
And you're fading away
They will still love you

Whoa, whoa, whoa...

Four hours later, after an easy and hazard-free journey, they were cantering by the training paddocks.

'Don't you think it's funny?' Holly said to the prince. 'We haven't seen a single witch.'

Prince Rupert shook his head. 'I have an idea Ghost Grindsniff is doing what he can to hold them at bay. But I doubt Grindsniff can work any of his magic much beyond the Grindsniff Wastelands. We must still watch our step.'

Celebrations

All thoughts of witches, skeleton horses and Red Vipereen vanished as soon as they passed inside the palace gates where it looked like everyone, even a sour-faced Liam had turned out to welcome them.

Bunting and fairy-lights were everywhere and, over the entrance, a huge banner...

WELCOME BACK

...and a brass band struck up a fanfare.

The only one Holly couldn't see was Schlox which she thought was a bit odd considering his most prized horse was back safe and sound.

Prince Rupert was clearly thinking along the same lines. 'Where is Schlox?' he demanded. 'Is he ill?'

The band stopped playing and there was a deathly hush until Madame Fosse stepped forward in a jingle jangly flurry.

'I don't know when or how you got the better of Red Vipereen but, at some point, my Diviner became crystal clear. I was able to knit together the whole dreadful story.

'It seems Schlox was in cahoots with Red Vipereen all along. I never did like the look of that man, and I should have trusted my instincts. In an effort to get his hands on the stables and put a stop to the Mission to find the Blessed Crystal, Vipereen enlisted the help of Schlox. Got him to apply for the post of trainer and no doubt arranged for him to have excellent references.

'The minute I grasped what had occurred, I confronted Schlox. Of course, he denied everything. So, without him knowing, I slipped a truth potion into his drink and within minutes he was confessing to being Red Vipereen's accomplice. As we all know, Grindsniff's Permanent Seal Spell made it impossible for Red Vipereen to gain direct access to the palace or the palace grounds. The PSS would have prevented him entering in person or by magic. The only way he could infiltrate the palace was by having access to a resident's mind. And Schlox was only too happy to go along with things, especially as Vipereen promised to make him his second-in-command once they got possession of the stables.

'Schlox wasn't at all keen on making the horses ill,' he told me, 'but Vipereen assured him there would be no lasting effects. You see, Schlox really does worship the horses. It's just that he wanted complete control over them so much, he was prepared to do anything.'

'Was it Vipereen who made me ill after the race? Edwin asked.

Madame Fosse nodded. 'Through Schlox, Vipereen was able to inject evil spirits into your mind. And, of course, it was Vipereen who got Schlox to drug the guards so that Black of Saingland could be abducted.'

'What I can't understand,' Holly said, 'is why Schlox was trying to blame Mulch for poisoning the horses.'

Prince Rupert smiled. 'The oldest trick in the world. Point the finger at someone else to avert suspicion. But where is Schlox? Where is the blackguard?'

'I had him locked in the cellar dungeon,' Madame Fosse said, 'but, no doubt with Vipereen's help he managed to get into the guards' minds to help him escape.'

'One more thing,' Prince Rupert said. 'Did Schlox say anything about Grindsniff?'

'I asked him, of course. But it seems that Schlox had nothing to do with Grindsniff's disappearance. Don't forget Grindsniff took himself off some time before Schlox arrived at the stables. I'm quite satisfied that Schlox was not involved in Grindsniff's disappearance and has no idea what has become of the wizard.'

'I think we have the answer to that,' Prince Rupert said quietly. The whole palace listened intently as the prince told of Holly and Edwin being helped by Grindsniff's ghost. 'I am also quite certain that Grindsniff played a big part in our safe return.'

Madame Fosse looked thoughtful. 'You realise, I hope, that Grindsniff as a ghost will never be able to utilise his full wizardry powers.'

Prince Rupert nodded. 'I rather thought that might be the case. All we can hope is that we find someone soon who is good enough to fill old Grindsniff's shoes. Grindsniff was at times foolish, but he was never disloyal.

But, for the time being, thanks largely to Holly and Edwin we have Black, our beloved Mission horse, back. This calls for a celebration, I think.'

A special banquet was arranged with Holly and Edwin as guests of honour. Holly wore a dark green velvet dress and matching headband, Edwin a black velvet suit complete with white shirt and black bow tie.

A big surprise awaited them in the banqueting hall. REAL FOOD. Real Food was unheard of at the palace, but Prince Rupert had decided to relax the palace rules on this one occasion. Holly and Edwin were both agreed, for once, that there was nothing like *seeing* roast beef and Yorkshire pudding with roast potatoes, Brussels sprouts, carrots and lashings of gravy and trifle and ice-cream. There was also real wine for the adults and orange or coke for the children.

Prince Rupert proposed a toast: 'To Holly and Edwin, our honoured guests, without whom we would never have recovered Black of Saingland.' The honoured guests nearly died with embarrassment as silver goblets were raised.

'And maybe one more toast,' the prince added. 'To Wizard Grindsniff, our absent friend, for the part he too played in helping us rescue Black of Saingland.'

Throughout the meal they were entertained by jesters and jugglers and a small band. Bonkers was laughing so much it was hard to know whether he was drunk or just madder than normal. Madame Fosse, sitting beside The Leper, had definitely had too much to drink. Drenched in jewellery and laughing non-stop, the resident psychic jangled so much she nearly drowned out the band.

After the meal, everyone made their way to the palace ballroom with its mirror-glass walls and sparkling chandeliers. Prince Rupert led Holly onto the floor for the first dance. Holly had never been good at dancing, but with the prince guiding her, she found herself gliding around the floor with ease.

Edwin, who was also useless at dancing, did a sort of shuffle around the floor with Madame Fosse who, although jangly, was surprisingly very graceful, Holly also danced with Mistoses, or at least, tried to dance with the palace secretary, who couldn't stop bouncing around and leaping in the air.

When, a little later, Patrick asked Holly for a dance, she was surprised to see all his spots had disappeared. His hair was slicked back and for the first time, he wasn't wearing glasses.

'Of course, I can't see a thing without them,' he admitted, as they shuffled around the floor, 'so you'll have to let me know if we're about to bump into anything.'

'You look very smart,' Holly said.

'Do you think so... Mm. Well, you look very pretty.'

'Don't be daft.' Holly giggled.

'I mean it, 'Patrick said. 'And there was something I wanted to ask you.'

'What? Whether eating carrots makes your hair red?'

'No, nothing like that. Mm. Well...I don't know...maybe...'

'Are you going to take all day, or what?'

Patrick took a deep breath. 'When we're a bit older, I was wondering if, er...you'd marry me?'

Holly was so shocked, she stumbled and would probably have fallen over, if Patrick hadn't caught her. *What was she supposed to say?* And then Holly remembered reading somewhere that girls weren't supposed to accept a proposal the first time.

'I'll have to think about it,' she said, trying to sound very cool and hoping Patrick wouldn't notice that her face was as red as her hair.

By the time the evening drew to a close, everyone was feeling that the dark clouds that had been hanging over the palace for so long had finally lifted.

Home Time

Holly had mixed feelings about leaving. 'Can't we stay for just a big longer?' she said.

'You can always come back,' Prince Rupert said. 'Don't worry, we will see you again. The palace will be forever in your debt.'

'Come along, come along,' Mistoses said. 'Madame Fosse is waiting to see you in her Psychitoreum before you go.'

Arms outstretched, Madame Fosse bustled towards them, jingling from head to toe and Holly and Edwin found themselves clasped to the psychic's ample bosom.

'Whatever shall we do without you?' she cried, finally releasing them. 'I tried, you know, to keep track of you throughout your perilous journey, but my Diviner kept letting me down. Red Vipereen's spell is still upon us. But now, thanks to you, we have Black of Saingland back and we can once again plan for the Mission to find the Blessed Crystal. Only then will we be certain of everlasting safety.'

Holly and Edwin handed back the horseshoes, pony brasses and necklaces. 'They were brilliant,' Holly said. 'Think we'd have been dead without them.' She paused. 'What about the wishes we made. What will happen now?'

'Whatever you wished for will come true very soon. But remember what I told you. On no account must you tell anyone what you wished for. At least not until your wishes comes true.' She handed back the necklaces. 'It might be as well to hang on to these, my dears. Just in case. And remember this, Vipereen is a clever magician, but he is nowhere near as powerful as Grindsniff once was. If you're bold enough, you can always call Vipereen's bluff.'

Full of beans, Mistoses led them to the stables where the rest of the palace was assembled to see them off.

Cate presented each of them with a book. For Holly, an adventure story – '*Jayne of Greystokes Stables*' and for Edwin, '*Champion Horses Down the Ages*'.

The Leper solemnly shook hands and wished them both good health. Bonkers, in a corner all by himself, was a gibbering wreck and no one could make out whether he was ecstatic at having Black back or sad because Holly and Edwin were leaving.

Finally, Prince Rupert stepped forward. 'Normally we would require you to suck a forget sweet before you leave,' he said, 'but for once we're going to make an exception. But you must promise not to divulge anything about The Mission to anyone, not even your closest friends and relatives.'

We haven't said goodbye to the horses.' Edwin said, tears welling.

On reaching the stables, they went from horse to horse. Holly flung her arms around Grey of Maccha. 'Goodbye Grey. Love you. I'll never forget you. Maybe I'll be able to come again.' Close to tears herself, Holly forced herself not to cry because of everyone watching. Edwin had to be torn away from Fury and Black because Mistoses was waiting to escort them to the shuttle that would transport them to the lift shaft.

Everyone was waving. 'Goodbye, goodbye. Good luck.'

When they reached the green gate leading onto the High Street, Mistoses pulled out a handkerchief and blew his nose.

'Thank you for everything,' Holly said.

'My privilege,' Mistoses wiped a tear from his eye and, without another word, disappeared inside the shed.

Stepping through the green gate, Holly and Edwin were dazzled by bright sunshine. The world they'd just left was now like a different planet. Waiting right outside at the kerbside was the stretch limo with Charles Reilly at the wheel. He stepped out and tipped his cap before ushering them inside.

'Wait till we tell Uncle Tom and Aunt Bridget what happened,' Edwin said.

'I shouldn't go on about everything that happened,' Holly warned. 'If they think it was dangerous, they won't let us go there again. And remember, we can't mention the wishes or The Mission.'

It was early evening by the time Holly and Edwin arrived back at Cherry Tree Cottage. Expecting to be welcomed with open arms by their aunt and uncle, imagining sinking into cosy warmth, they were shocked to find the small cottage had been wrecked, the thatched roof blown off, all the windows broken and the front door hanging off its hinges.

'D'you think it was a storm?' Edwin said.

Holly shook her head. She plucked a ragged piece of fishnet tights off a rosebush in the front garden. 'Look, the witches did this.'

They dashed into the house and went from one room to another. Edwin even looked down the cellar. But there was no sign of their aunt and uncle.

Edwin started crying. 'What d'you think has happened to them? They've disappeared. Just like Mum.'

'I'm not sure, but I have an idea.'

Charles Reilly was standing by the limo looking shocked. 'Can you take us to Barford?' Holly said.

'Certainly, miss. My orders were to carry out your every wish.'

'Why are we going there?' Edwin asked.

'Because I bet that's where our aunt and uncle are. At the Holding Bay.'

Secrets of the Holding Bay

There was only one problem. Holly had no idea where the Holding Bay was. As they drove around Barford she racked her brains trying to remember the route they'd taken after making their escape. Round and round the town they went so that it was long after midnight before they stumbled upon Holding Bay house, looking even more uglier than Holly remembered.

'Now what?' Edwin said. 'We're going to be caught by the witches. We shouldn't have come here.'

'Leave everything to me, Holly said.

'Do you think you can wait for us?' Holly asked the chauffeur.

'Of course, but I hope you know what you're doing, miss.'

'Don't worry, I know exactly what I'm doing. Do you have anything sharp in the car? Like a knife?'

Charles Reilly produced a Swiss penknife.

'Great. Anything else sharp?'

'Mmm.' The chauffeur rooted around in the glove compartment. 'These any good?' He held up a pair of scissors.

'Perfect. Best if you wait at the end of the street, Mr Reilly and if we're not out in twenty minutes, call the police or Prince Rupert.' Holly turned to her brother. 'Now you follow me. We're going round the back of the house.'

'What for?'

'Sshh.'

Around the back of the house, they found rows and rows of Harley Davidsons parked up for the night. Holly handed her brother the scissors. 'We have to get to work on the tyres. Okay. Make sure the witches can't catch us if we have to make a quick get-away.'

There were so many bikes it took ages. All the while, Holly kept one eye on the house, just in case a witch happened to look out of a window and spot them.

'Now we've got to get into the house,' Holly said.

'How do we do that? Knock on the front door?'

'Don't be stupid,' Holly said. 'We get in the same way as we escaped. Look there's the drainpipe. Up you go.'

'But we can't go inside,' Edwin protested.

'How else are we going to rescue Uncle Tom and Aunt Bridget? We've still got the necklaces that Madame Fosse gave us, don't forget.'

'But you don't even know that they're inside. I thought they just caught children.'

'They have prisoners as well. Remember Emily and Michael telling us about the witches keeping prisoners in the cellar.'

'We'll end up in the cellar ourselves, most likely,' Edwin said.

'No, we won't. Now, come on, we can't hang around all night.'

No sooner had Edwin shinned up the drainpipe, than Holly followed and led the way over the flat roof to the bathroom window. She held her breath, hoping and praying it was still unlocked. It was.

Once inside, Holly crept over to the door opening onto the corridor and peered out. It was pitch black, so she couldn't see much, but she reckoned the witches would already have made their night inspection. The nightly inspection always took place around midnight and it was well past midnight now. The witches would have gone back to bed for the night. Very slowly and quietly, Holly led the way along the corridor, past the children's bedroom, to the top of the stairs. The stairs creaked so much she expected a witch to appear any minute. The stairs seemed never ending as they inched their way down in the dark. Off the hall, to the right, near the kitchen, Holly recalled there was a door that led down to the cellar.

It was hard to see in the dark, but Holly made out two stout bolts.

Trying not to make a noise, she slid back one bolt, then the other. The door creaked a bit as they opened it. Immediately in front of them was a narrow and steep set of stairs. Holly drew Edwin in next to her on the top step, closed the door and fumbled for a light switch on the wall. The light was very feeble, but it was better than nothing.

Holly led the way down the rickety steps. The cellar light was so dim she couldn't make out much apart from a few shapes lying on the floor. She crept nearer to the shapes, which she could now see were people, and, as her eyes grew used to the dark, she gasped. Lying fast asleep side by side were Uncle Tom and Aunt Bridget all tied up and gagged, but it was the person next to them that made Holly gasp.

'Mum, Mum,' Edwin shouted, before Holly could stop him.

Holly got to work immediately freeing first Mum and then the others.

'Oh, Holly, Edwin,' Alice Goodchild was on her feet, tears streaming down her face.

Edwin threw himself into his mother's arms. 'I kept thinking you were dead, Mum,' he said.

'How long have you been here?' Holly said.

'I've lost track of time,' Alice said. 'I knew they'd captured you as well. One of the witches told me. I felt so helpless. I thought I'd never see the two of you ever again.' She held her arms out to Holly.

'Holly gave her Mum a quick kiss. She wanted to shout for joy only there wasn't time for any of that. Any minute now a witch might appear. Someone had to keep a cool head.

'Wimbally, wombally, will you look at the pair of you,' Aunt Bridget said. 'I couldn't stop blaming myself for letting you go off and then the witches came and here's where we've ended up.'

Uncle Tom was too busy wiping tears from his eyes to say or do anything.

'We mustn't make a noise,' Holly warned. 'The witches...' But her warning came too late because right at that moment, several witches came clattering down the cellar steps.

'You've come back, then,' one of the witches cackled.

Holly yanked her necklace free and waved it at the witches. Immediately, they staggered back a few feet.

'Edwin,' Holly called. 'Your necklace.'

The two of them twirled their necklaces for all they were worth, the power from their combined efforts sending the witches flying.

'Quick, quick, all of you,' Holly said. 'Up the stairs. Turn right and through the kitchen. We might be able to get out the back door.

Holly had no sooner bolted the cellar door than she heard the two witches thundering back up the stairs and, as she was racing through the kitchen, she heard them hammering on the cellar door.

Uncle Tom had the back door open, but already the rest of the Holding Bay witches were on the move, cackling and pounding their way toward the kitchen.

'Go round to the car,' Holly yelled to Edwin tell Mr Reilly to wait. There's something else I've got to do then I'll catch you up.'

'I'm not going without you, Holly,' Alice said.

'Please,' Holly begged. 'Go with Edwin. I know what I'm doing.'

Holly went back into the kitchen and was just in time to tuck herself into a dark corner when the witches burst through the door. They streamed past her making horrible noises in their throats. Holly had to stop herself sneezing there was so much dust around.

No sooner had the last witch disappeared out of the back door, than Holly made her way back through the house and up the stairs. From outside she could hear the witches screaming on finding their tyres slashed. Holly raced along the upstairs landing and rushed into the children's bedroom. 'Wake up, wake up' she yelled.

She shook Emily and Michael. 'Come on, quick. You're getting out'

The children were all now wide awake and rubbing their eyes.

'What's happening?'

'What, what, where am I?'

'Is there a fire?'

What are you doing back, Holly?' Emily was out of bed and starting to get dressed.

'No time to get dressed.' Holly shouted. 'Follow me, I promise you'll be safe.'

Leading the way, she tore back along the corridor to the stairs trying, at the same time, to work out what to do next. It was no use climbing out of the bathroom room and onto the flat roof or even going out the back door. The witches would be onto them in no time. And when they reached the street, where on earth were they going to go. Cherry Tree cottage was a wreck.

Hurtling down the stairs, the children, in their pyjamas, hot on her heels, Holly saw Aunt Winifred in her dressing-gown standing at the bottom.

'What's going on, Holly dear?' Aunt Winifred said.

'We've got to get out,' Holly said. 'The house is about to collapse any minute. The witches told me to get you and the other children out as quickly as possible. Where's the key to the front door?'

'Oh my, oh my,' Aunt Winifred looked confused.

'The key,' Holly said. 'To the front door. Quick.'

'I have one, right here, dear,' Aunt Winifred said, pulling out a key from her pocket.'

Holly struggled with the bolts before ramming the key in the lock and turning it. Out in the street, she could see the limo at the end of the street, but an even more welcoming sight met her eyes. Galloping towards the Holding Bay, like hounds from hell, was a team of horses. It couldn't possibly be... but it was – all the palace horses headed by Prince Rupert on Black of Saingland, Greton on Hercules and Mistoses and the palace guards not far behind.

'Run, run,' Holly shouted to everyone, but Aunt Winifred was finding it hard to walk, let alone run. Not that it mattered because the horses were on their way; also, Charles Reilly was driving towards them.

Holly had just decided they were going to make it when the Holding Bay witches came hurtling round the side of the house on foot and in the sky, a lightning flash, followed by another flash, heralded the arrival of Red Vipereen. He loomed in the sky, a red glow, an extraordinary figure with a flowing beard and snake eyes flinging red darts. He twirled around, once, twice, three times and disappeared leaving a great wall of fire, a roaring sheet of flames, giving out an intense heat, and separating the children from the horses and the limo.

Close to despair, Holly recalled something Madame Fosse had said. "If you're bold enough, you can always call Vipereen's bluff". At the same time, an image came to mind of the fiery hoops at the Shergar Obstacle Race and sailing safely through the hoops on Nessa.

The children had turned around ready to run back straight into the arms of the witches. Seeing the witches, Aunt Winifred was thoroughly discombobulated and couldn't decide which way to go.

'Stop,' Holly shouted at the top of lungs. 'The fire's only a magic fire. It won't hurt you...' The children looked back, stopped dead, and watched as Holly, eyes closed, leapt right into the centre of the red-hot flames. For a few moments, the heat burned her cheeks and scorched her arms and legs. But then, miraculously, she found she'd landed unscathed the other side and right there, in front of her, was Prince Rupert, together with Mistoses and the palace guards.

'Quick, you must help. The fire won't hurt you,' Without another word, Holly leapt back through the flames.

The children and the witches were all standing stock-still in amazement, but not for long. The witches, recovering quickly, resumed their screaming and ran to grab hold of the children. At the same time, the palace guards came hurtling through the flames and as a scuffle broke out between the witches and the guards, Holly had time to get all the children and Aunt Winifred, who seemed to have completely lost her mind, through the wall of fire.

While Tom Goodchild immediately took charge of Aunt Winifred and the children helping them all pile into the limo, Holly and Edwin mounted Grey and Fury. They were getting ready to persuade the horses to jump through the fire when, just as quickly as it had flared up, the fire vanished, and they had a clear view of the fierce fighting between witches and palace guards.

'Come on, come on,' Edwin yelled before leading a charge into the battle scene. The horses reared up and struck out at the witches, hooves flailing. Screams of pain mingled with the triumphant whinnying of the horses. Noses jabbing and nails clawing, the witches weren't giving in without a struggle, but they were no match for the horses' pounding hooves. They fell back before turning and fleeing for the cover of the Holding Bay.

A further signal from the prince and all the horses and riders retreated, racing back to catch up with the crawling limo.

Holly brought Grey alongside Prince Rupert and Mistoses. 'Where are we going?'

The prince smiled. 'A surprise,' he said. 'A nice one, I hope.'

'It's no use us going back to Cherry Tree Cottage. It's been wrecked by the witches.'

'So, Madame Fosse gave me to understand. Her Diviner was behaving itself for once and she picked up on the danger you were in and what had happened to the cottage. We were already on our way when we received a call from Charles Reilly.'

'So where are we going?'

'You'll soon see,' Mistoses chortled.

The prince, it turned out, had reserved enough rooms for them all at the Swan Hotel. And he made it plain that they were to stay there for as long as it took for Cherry Tree Cottage to be repaired and for the Holding Bay children to be found homes with relatives. As for Aunt Winifred, Prince Rupert promised her a permanent home at the palace.

'Enjoy your stay and order anything you want. The palace will pay for everything of course including the repairs to the cottage.'

When Aunt Bridget protested, the prince silenced her. 'My dear, Mrs. Goodchild, I cannot tell you how much the palace is in your debt. Nothing could ever repay Holly and Edwin for what they have done for the palace.'

The prince continued. 'My one regret is that I could not accommodate you all at the palace. But you see, we are having to take extra precautions. In any case, you may be safer at the hotel than at the palace. I do hope you understand.'

'Well…oh…my…Wimbally, wombally,' was all Aunt Bridget could get out.

The prince also arranged for his palace guards to be posted both inside and outside the Swan Hotel.

'Until the palace finds a Powers of Darkness Adversary we cannot relax our guard,' the prince told Holly and Edwin before leaving the hotel. 'You must watch your every step. For the time being Red Vipereen has retreated to lick his wounds, but I very much doubt he's going to give up that easily.'

Holly and Edwin, in fact everyone enjoyed their stay at the five-star hotel immensely. Alice Goodchild, Holly and Edwin shared the best suite in the hotel while Tom and Bridget had one of the other suites. The children from the Holding Bay had a room each. Compared to what they'd been used to for so long, it was the height of luxury. Not only that, but the day after they had booked into the hotel, a special delivery was made of clothes in varying sizes, enough for everyone to pick and choose.

'It's brillo,' Michael said, pushing his specs up his nose. 'Wish I could stay here permanently.'

'You were great, Holly,' Emily said. 'We might have been stuck at the Holding Bay forever. The meals are fantastic.' And so they were. Each morning they had an English breakfast, every afternoon, they all tucked into high tea and in the evening, they were served with a three-course meal and waited on hand and foot.

'D'you remember, Holly?' Edwin said one day 'how Dad used to say that he'd treat us to high tea at the Swan? Well, here we are having high tea every single day.'

Neither Holly nor Edwin said anything and nor did their Mum, but they couldn't stop thinking how sad it was that Dad wasn't with them to enjoy it all.

One by one, all the Holding Bay the children were contacted and collected by relatives, one or two from far-flung corners of the globe. Michael, Emily and a quiet boy called Peter who didn't say much but ate a lot, were the only ones remaining when news arrived via the palace messenger boy that Cherry Tree cottage was ready for occupation and could the Goodchild family be ready to leave at four o'clock that afternoon.

'Do we take all the lovely clothes with us, I wonder?' Alice asked her sister-in-law.

'Of course,' Aunt Bridget said. 'I can't see the prince wanting them back. It's one of his treats. He's very rich.'

At a quarter to four, they were all packed up and waiting in the hotel foyer to be picked up. Michael and Emily were there to see them off.

'Hope you're soon in touch with your relatives,' Holly said.

'I don't mind staying here for the rest of my life,' Michael said. 'The only thing that bothers me is being caught by the witches again and taken back to the Holding Bay.'

Emily hugged Holly and Edwin. 'I've had a letter from a cousin in New Zealand. It looks like I might be going to stay with her. I'll let you know. I'll write to you,' she said.

When Charles Reilly pulled up outside Cherry Tree Cottage, 69 Green Lane, they all thought they'd arrived at the wrong house. It was twice the size it had been. Even bigger than the Cherry Tree pub next door.

And much to their astonishment, Prince Rupert came sauntering out of the front door to greet them.

'Welcome home,' he said. 'I do hope the work meets with your approval.'

'This can't be our little cottage,' Bridget said. 'It's more the size of a hotel.'

Prince Rupert coughed. 'Er...I hope you don't mind, but I took the liberty of having the cottage extended. I thought...er, that you might all rather like to share the house. Of course, if you'd rather not...'

'That's a wonderful idea,' Uncle Tom said. 'Alice, Holly, Edwin, how about it? Think you can put up with the two of us?'

The smiles on the faces of Alice and her children said it all.'

'There's only a lick of paint needed, to the outside. Well maybe more than a lick. I've arranged for pots of paints to be used that Wizard Grindsniff invested with special powers whilst he was with us. It will help ward off evil. Not that you should be in any danger,' he said quickly. 'You see, the witches will no longer pursue you. Having helped us regain Black, you should no longer be a threat to them.' He paused. 'Tomorrow then, there will be some workmen along to do the painting. I hope you won't find their presence inconvenient.'

He smiled and there was an expression on his face that Holly couldn't fathom.

Wishful Thinking

Worn out from their adventures, everyone was keen to have an early night but, strange to say, Holly couldn't get to sleep. She made her way to Edwin's room and found him wide awake as well.

'Do you wish you were back at the stables?' she asked. 'I mean you were so brilliant with the horses and everything.'

'It would be all right if Mum and Dad could be there. Uncle Tom and Aunt Bridget as well. I can't help thinking, what if Dad comes back? He'll go back to our old house and wonder where we are.'

'You know what?' Holly said, 'I'd forgotten all about the wish I made.'

'So had I. I wished…'

Holly clamped a hand over his mouth. 'Don't say a word. Remember what Madame Fosse said. We weren't to tell anyone what we wished for. Not until the wish came true. I'd better get back to bed, or else you might start to say something you shouldn't.'

It was so late when the pair of them finally got to sleep, that they would probably have slept until midday but for a great commotion going on outside. Edwin came into Holly's room rubbing his eyes. 'What's all that noise? It's coming from the back garden.'

'Must be some workmen finishing things.' Holly clambered over her bed to look out of her window that overlooked the back garden. Sure enough, three workmen were busy unloading tins of paint from the back of a flatbed truck. But it wasn't the workmen or what they were doing that riveted her attention. It was the sight of a great hulk of a man, a giant of a man you might say, who was directing operations.

Holly's shrieks had Edwin climbing up beside her. A huge grin spread across his face.

Up and dressed, Alice Goodchild was already racing over the lawn, and Holly beat Edwin to the kitchen door by a whisker.

'Dad, Dad,' they chorused.

Jack Goodchild stood there grinning. His wife and children piled into his open arms. They were all laughing and crying at the same time, making such a commotion it brought Tom and Bridget out.

'My, oh my. Will you look who's here. Oh, wimbally, wombally. Come inside Jack. Come inside all of you and have some toast and a cup of tea.'

'Did you make lots of money, Dad?' Edwin wanted to know when they were all sat round the kitchen table.

'Er, not exactly,' Dad said sheepishly. 'I was in the coldest, most remote spot you can imagine. No communication links for starters, so there was no way I could contact you. It was a good month or so, before

I even got paid. In the end I couldn't stand worrying about you all. When I got back to Barford I found a note pinned to the door informing me you were all at Cherry Tree Cottage and inviting me to apply for the post of foreman with Stone and Coates, a firm of decorators here in Strawbridge. I didn't have much to lose, so I went after the job and blow me if they didn't turn round and offer it there and then. And to cap it all, the very first job I was given was this one.

'Wimbally, wombally,' Aunt Bridget exclaimed.

'I think Prince Rupert must have had a hand in things' Holly said.

'Prince Rupert? Who on earth is Prince Rupert, Tink?'

'We've got loads to tell you, Dad,' Holly said.

'And now that it's happened, sis, I can tell you what I wished for, 'Edwin said. 'I wished for Mum and Dad to come home. Bet that's what you wished for as well.'

'Is someone going to tell me what all this is about?' Dad said.

'And what's all this about wishes?' Mum wanted to know.

'Go on then, Edwin, you tell them all about what happened,' Holly said. 'Except don't forget, you're not to mention you know what.'

'No, you tell them.'

'And exactly what is *you know what?*' Aunt Bridget demanded.

'That's the only bit we can't tell you,' Holly said.

In the end, they told the story between them.

Jack Goodchild wiped tears from his eyes. 'I always knew you were special, the two of you,' he said. 'I knew it all along.'

'Except Edwin is the really special one,' Holly said, but she said it so quietly, no one heard.

Lightning Source UK Ltd.
Milton Keynes UK
UKHW010742090522
402649UK00001B/10